The Book of One Hundred Truths

☆

The Book of
One Hundred Truths

☆

JULIE SCHUMACHER

SCHOLASTIC INC.
New York Toronto London Auckland Sydney
Mexico City New Delhi Hong Kong Buenos Aires

ISBN-13: 978-0-545-10900-0
ISBN-10: 0-545-10900-0

Copyright © 2006 by Julie Schumacher. All rights reserved.
Published by Scholastic Inc., 557 Broadway, New York, NY 10012, by arrangement with Delacorte Press, an imprint of Random House Children's Books, a division of Random House, Inc. SCHOLASTIC and associated logos are trademarks and/or registered trademarks of Scholastic Inc.

12 11 10 9 8 7 6 5 4 3 2   9 10 11 12 13 14/0

Printed in the U.S.A.   40

First Scholastic Book Club printing, March 2009

The text of this book is set in 12-point Goudy.
Book design by Trish Parcell Watts

Thanks to all who assisted in the creation of this book:

My editor, the indefatigable Jodi Keller (Congratulations on your wedding!)

My agent, Lisa Bankoff, and her daughter Charlotte Ruth Simms

My husband, Lawrence Jacobs, the most optimistic political scientist in North America

My daughters—Emma, who took pen in hand to notice what others had overlooked; and Bella, who loyally championed the first version of the manuscript but is willing to stand by the revised copy also

Alison McGhee, dearest friend and reader

The miraculous members of Women Who Wine, who offer encouragement and hilarity and solace, and who will find themselves inscribed, with the author's gratitude, within these pages

For my mother, Winifred Temple Schumacher,
who taught me to love the ocean and the written word

☆

CHAPTER ONE

☆

Probably because they didn't trust me, my parents were grilling me at the airport in Minneapolis, asking all the usual travel questions. Did I have my backpack? *Yes.* Did I have the claim check for my suitcase? *Yes.* Did I need to use the bathroom?

"Guess what? They have bathrooms on planes now," I said.

My father patted his pockets. "Do you need any chewing gum?"

"I already have some."

"A bottle of water?"

"Dad," I said. "This is kind of insulting."

"Okay, I'll stop. A magazine?"

Every summer since I was six years old, my parents had been sending me to visit my father's relatives at the beach in New Jersey. They were always more anxious about it than I was. I liked eating lunch on the plane at thirty thousand feet, and I liked staying at my grandparents' house, which was full of lumpy, mismatched furniture and old-fashioned wallpaper that would have been seriously ugly anywhere else.

Yes, I said. I had a magazine. I had absolutely everything that a person going on a plane could possibly want.

But then my mother cleared her throat, opened a shopping bag I hadn't noticed, and offered me a notebook. It was light blue, with thick, heavy unlined paper— a much nicer notebook than the kind I used at school.

"What's that for?" I felt uneasy. I was already bringing a lot of things with me: a gift for my grandparents, a lunch and some junk food, my CD player and a dozen CDs, and several books that my father insisted I would want to read.

"It's a notebook of truths," my mother said. She flipped the pages of the notebook and held it toward me. "You can write anything you want in here, as long as every single thing you write is true."

"What do you mean, *every single thing?*" I looked at the notebook but didn't touch it. On its cover was a white star about the size of my fingertip. All around us, people were pushing strollers and dragging suitcases toward their gates.

"Well, I'm not talking about essays, or even paragraphs," my mother said. She was standing very close to me; I could smell peppermint on her breath. "I'm only talking about observations. Write a few sentences at first. You can make a list."

"Gee. A list." I shifted my backpack to my other shoulder. "That sounds exciting."

My mother didn't appreciate sarcasm. "Notebooks are private," she went on. I was almost exactly her height, and she was looking at me forehead to forehead, eye to eye. "That's the best thing about them. You can write down any truths at all. Anything you're thinking."

"The world is round," I said. "How's that for a truth?"

My mother tucked her hair behind her ears and said that *the world is round* was a fact instead of a truth, and that there was a difference. She said she suspected I knew what it was.

"Time to get on that plane," my father said. He clapped his hands.

Here was a truth: my father didn't like goodbyes. He didn't like train stations or bus depots or airports. I could tell he was nervous by the way he had been jingling the change in his pockets.

A tall blond woman ran over my foot with her rolling suitcase.

"We have one more minute," my mother said. She straightened the sleeve of my T-shirt and pulled me aside. "You'll be gone for three weeks. Twenty-two days. If you write down four or five *true things* every day"—she tapped the cover of the notebook—"you'll have a hundred. A hundred true things."

"A hundred," I repeated. I had to admit that *one hundred truths* had a certain ring to it.

"You'll feel better if you use this," my mother said. "You never know what you might discover. You might learn something new." Her green eyes were like matching traffic lights. "You might find out something new about who you are."

I didn't want to get into that kind of discussion. I took the notebook. It felt good in my hands; the blue cover was soft.

"Off you go, then," my father said. He gave my ticket to the flight attendant, who wrapped a paper bracelet around my wrist as if I were two years old instead of almost thirteen.

I started down the carpeted hallway and waved. My parents, their arms around each other's shoulders, waved back.

"We'll see you soon," my father said. "Call us when you get there. And have a good time. Behave yourself."

I told him I would.

But I should probably mention something right now, before this story goes any further: my name is Theodora Grumman, and I am a liar.

CHAPTER TWO

☆

About three and a half hours later, I was in the back-seat of my aunt Celia's car, on the way to my Nenna and Granda's house in Port Harbor, New Jersey. My aunt Celia and my aunt Ellen—two of my father's four sisters—had signed for me as if I were a package when I got to the airport in Philadelphia. Now we were cruising down a narrow ribbon of road, my aunts arguing about the speed of the car, the amount of oil it was probably burning, and whether the warm air rushing through the windows would slow us down. Celia was driving, which meant that it was Ellen's job to criticize.

Another truth for my notebook: some of my father's relatives were crazy. They didn't chase each other around the house with carving knives, but they had what my Nenna called habits or quirks. My mother was an only child, like me, and she said that the polite word for people like my aunts was *eccentric*.

"What are you writing back there?" Celia asked. She glanced at me in the rearview mirror. She and Ellen were both large and sturdy, with gray-blue eyes. They looked like meat packers, my father said. Celia worked as a hotel manager, and Ellen was the principal at an elementary school. I felt sorry for all the kindergartners she probably terrified every September.

"Nothing." I zipped up my backpack and put it on the floor of the car by my feet.

"You were writing something. I saw you. In a little blue notebook."

"I don't have a notebook," I said.

In front of me, in the passenger seat, my aunt Ellen twitched. Her neck was tan and as thick as a column.

I sniffed at the air pouring in through the window, but there was no beach smell yet. My grandparents—Nenna and Granda—lived right on the ocean, and every summer when I went to visit, I tried to pinpoint the moment when the smell of farmland and manure gave way to salt and water. As soon as I smelled it, I felt I was up to my ankles in hot soft sand, the ocean spread out in front of me like a living blanket.

"Can I have the back bedroom again?" I asked. "The one with the porch?" I always slept in the back bedroom. It was small, and I had to walk through my grandparents' room to reach it, but I thought it was the nicest room in the house. It was shaped like the letter *L,* and instead of beds, it had two berths in it, like hammocks, that clipped to the wall when no one was using them. My Granda liked to sleep in them sometimes, before he got too old. He said it reminded him of being in the navy.

"No, sorry, you can't. It's already spoken for," Celia said. "We've got a full house this summer."

"What do you mean, a full house?" Even though my grandparents' house filled up with relatives on Saturdays and Sundays, weekdays were usually slow and lonely. I'd been looking forward to that kind of loneliness—to spending time by myself without anyone prodding me or saying, "Why don't you get up off that couch and call a friend?"

A truck was coming toward us in the opposite lane. Celia jerked her elbow up and down; the truck driver honked. "What I mean, Thea," she said, chewing on a toothpick, "is that Liam and Austin have the back bedroom. They got here first."

"Liam and Austin? Why are they sleeping over?" Liam and Austin were my aunt Ellen's sons, fifteen and seventeen—my oldest cousins. Their father had died when they were little, and they lived with my aunt Ellen about ten miles away from my Nenna and Granda.

"Because both of them are working at the hoagie shop this summer—the Breakers," Ellen said. "If they sleep at home, I'll have to drive them to work every day. But if they stay at your Nenna and Granda's, they can walk up the street."

We drove past some cornfields, a fruit and honey stand, and half a dozen signs for Jersey's finest tomatoes.

"So I guess that means I'll be in the middle room," I said. "The one with the seashell wallpaper."

There were four bedrooms on the second floor of my grandparents' house: one belonged to my Nenna and Granda; one was Celia's (she was older than my father but had never left home); and the one with the porch and the swinging berths was now Liam and Austin's. I didn't like the seashell room as much, but I supposed if it was the only one left (my parents were always telling me that I should be flexible), it was mine.

Celia adjusted her rearview mirror so she could see me. "Actually, the seashell room is going to be Edmund's this year," she said.

"Edmund's?" Edmund was another cousin, my aunt Trisha's four-year-old son. He and his seven-year-old sister, Jocelyn, masqueraded as the world's most well-behaved children. They said please and thank you about every two minutes. I remembered that the summer before, Jocelyn had told me that her favorite thing in the world was making beds. "Then where am I supposed to sleep?" I asked.

"Upstairs. Up on the third floor," Ellen said.

A sprinkler the size of a football field crept like a long-legged robot through the furrows of dirt beside the road.

"The only problem with that idea," I said slowly, "is

that *there is no third floor*. Do you mean the attic?" The last time I'd been in my Nenna and Granda's attic, it had been full of moths. Every step sent a ragged little cloud of them up from the carpet. They were like feathery halos around my feet.

"Don't worry, we fixed it up. It looks much better now," Celia said. "Oops." She jerked her elbow up and down for another truck. "We tore out the rugs, for starters. And cleared out some boxes and other whatnot. It's a little warm up there, I guess, but it isn't infested anymore. You'll be sharing it with Jocelyn."

"I wouldn't have used the word *infested*," Ellen said. "Would you please keep both of your hands on the wheel?"

"Wait a minute." I clutched the back of the driver's seat. "Did you say I have to share a room with Jocelyn?"

Ellen opened the glove compartment and started sifting through it. "This is a mess, Celia," she said. "Why do you have all these take-out menus? You don't actually eat at the Chicken Hut?"

I could feel my vacation being yanked out from under my feet. I didn't want to share a bedroom. Ever since I was six weeks old, I had had a room of my own. "Why are Jocelyn and Edmund staying over?" I asked. My parents and I were the only members of the family who didn't live near my Nenna and Granda. We slept at their house when we visited; everyone else could visit for the day.

"Their parents dropped them off," Ellen said. "They're in Europe. Trisha's leading a tour." My aunt Trisha was a travel agent.

"They're willing to pay you to do some babysitting," Celia said. "What did we decide on, Ellen? I don't remember. Two dollars an hour?"

"Two and a half or three," Ellen said. She took a rubber band from her wrist (she usually wore half a dozen) and fastened a stack of paper from the glove compartment together. "Mainly we're talking about afternoons. I think we've got the mornings covered. It'll be a good opportunity for you to—"

"Actually, I'm not allowed to babysit." The words came up from my throat before I knew what I was going to say. Lies were that easy. They slid past me like butter. "My parents don't let me."

Silence filled the front seat, as if someone had pumped it in through the air vents.

"They don't let you?" Ellen asked.

"I'm irresponsible," I said. "I might be a danger to myself or others."

"Your father didn't mention that on the phone," Ellen said. "I don't remember that he—"

"Leave it, Ellen." Celia stopped at a light. "We'll talk about it later."

"Well, you know we need someone to keep an eye on—"

"*Leave it*." Celia stepped on the gas and the car

jerked forward. "We should be there in about twenty minutes, Thea."

"Thirty. And it would be nice if we got there all in one piece," Ellen sniffed.

"Please shut up, Ellen," Celia said.

Ellen snapped the glove compartment closed, then rearranged the rubber bands on her wrist.

I leaned back against the seat and fell asleep to the sound of them quarreling, a back-and-forth as predictable as the tide.

CHAPTER THREE

☆

I didn't set out to become a liar. I knew the story about George Washington and his cherry tree and his little ax.

The first couple of serious lies I told almost made me sick. After I told them, I felt dizzy, as if I was halfway to throwing up.

But then it got easier. One lie led naturally to the next. And eventually the lies started to feel like helium balloons: I could tie them to things I didn't want to think about, then watch them rise into the air and float away.

"So—I hear you were born here in Minneapolis," said Mrs. Benitez, our new neighbor. It was early April and she and her family had just moved in. She had spotted me dragging a plastic bag full of kitchen scraps out to the trash cans in the alley, and she leaned over the fence that separated our two backyards. "I have two little boys who are looking forward to winter sports. Do you play hockey? Do you like to skate?"

"Actually, no." I paused by the fence, trash bag at my side. "I have an artificial leg," I said. "I can't."

"Oh, I'm so sorry." Mrs. Benitez wiped her hands. She'd been sprinkling salt on her sidewalk. "That must be difficult for you. But if it makes you feel any better, I wouldn't have noticed."

I told her not to be sorry; I was getting used to it. I told her that the new kind of leg I had actually fit very well.

"An *artificial leg*?" my mother asked a week or so later. She pointed out that I had already told another neighbor, Mrs. Guest, that I couldn't walk her dog because I wasn't allowed outdoors after four o'clock. My parents had been getting fairly strict, I had tried to explain. Mrs. Guest was surprised.

"Maybe Thea doesn't like dogs," my father suggested. "I'm not sure that we should force her to walk them."

"Dogs aren't the issue here," my mother insisted. "And neither are artificial legs." She put her fingers under my chin and forced me to look at her. "Is this some kind of phase you're going through? What's this about, anyway?"

I told her it wasn't *about* anything.

"Are you sure?"

Yes, I was sure. Other parents, I told my mother, probably *wished* their kids had more imagination.

About a week later I told my science teacher, Ms. Wang, that I had a learning disability. It wasn't serious, I explained, but my doctor thought it might help if I could sit at the back of the classroom next to the window, by myself.

"Thea?" my mother asked. She and Ms. Wang, it turned out, had run into each other at the grocery store. Who could have known they would shop on the same afternoon, at the very same place? Ms. Wang, my mother said, had suggested that I might benefit from several sessions with a counselor. Luckily, Ms. Wang had explained, there was a counselor I could meet with for free, and he worked at my school.

"What do you think?" my mother asked. She had her hands on her hips.

No way, I told her. There was nothing wrong with me, and I had no intention of talking to a counselor. Absolutely none.

☆

"Let's just start by getting acquainted," said Mr. Hanover, the counselor. "We'll spend some time talking here in my office, and I'll try to understand what you might be going through." Mr. Hanover was tall, way over six feet, and whenever he spoke, I ended up staring at his shoes. They were black and polished and enormous. I imagined them waiting patiently in his closet when he wasn't wearing them, at night. "How does that sound?" he asked. "Thea? Hello?" He wanted to know what I was thinking, just like my mother did.

"I'm not thinking anything," I told him. Actually, I was thinking that the only kids who got pulled out of class to see Mr. Hanover were the ones who set fires in the bathroom trash cans or carved their names into the bulletin boards with tacks. I got pulled out of class because Ms. Wang had run into my mother in the grocery store.

"It's all right to feel confused sometimes," Mr. Hanover said. His left shoe nudged a yellow paper clip across the carpet. "And I want you to know that you can speak to me about your feelings in perfect confidence."

"That's great," I said. He seemed to be waiting for me to say something else. "Thanks for telling me," I added.

"How are you getting along with your classmates?" The yellow paper clip disappeared beneath the sole of his shoe. "I hear there's been a little bit of tension."

"No, not really," I said. Mostly, the other kids didn't pay any attention to me. If I opened my mouth and said something that sounded like a lie—for example, that I wasn't allowed to complete the autobiography assignment because my parents felt that writing about myself would make me conceited—there might be a pause in the conversation, like a hole appearing suddenly at our feet, but then somebody else would start talking and the class would go on, and the hole would be covered with words.

I always knew that the hole was still there, though, pulsing and breathing underneath us. We walked right across it. We ignored it. We kept going.

"I understand that your parents are concerned about a number of tall tales that have gotten back to them. Am I right?" Mr. Hanover smiled. His smile was wide and creepy, as if the edges of his mouth were made of elastic. "There was something last week; let's see. . . ." He scanned his desk for a piece of paper. "You weren't able to participate in gym class because your religious beliefs don't allow for—"

"Relay races," I said. "I'm Episcopalian."

"Ah," said Mr. Hanover. "I suppose that explains it." We both stared at his shoes.

"School can be stressful." Mr. Hanover spoke to the spotted carpet between us. "But talking to someone about what you're experiencing can help quite a bit. A lot of people find that during difficult episodes of their lives, or even periods of trauma—"

"I have to be getting back to class now," I said. "I think we have a test coming up. I need to study."

"But you didn't let me finish my sentence." The toe of his right shoe moved slowly up and down.

"You can finish it next time," I said.

But I tried to make sure that there wasn't a next time. When Ms. Wang called me to the front of the class a few days later and handed me a slip of paper that read, *Appt w/ Mr. Hanover,* I told her I didn't know anyone by that name.

"Room 107," Ms. Wang whispered. She was trying to be subtle. *Room 107* had a reputation. "On the first floor," she added. "Near the main office."

I told her I had no idea in the world where that was.

CHAPTER FOUR

☆

Truth #1: My father doesn't like goodbyes.

Truth #2: Most Grummans are weird. Some are weirder than others.

Truth #3: I don't know what to write in this notebook.

Celia and Ellen and I pulled into the driveway at two-fifteen. "Home sweet home," Celia said. "Thea? Do you need help with your bags?"

"No, I'm coming." I got out of the car. The air was thick and wet and salty. Not like the air in Minneapolis, which smelled like trees.

I grabbed my suitcase. My grandparents' house loomed in front of us. It looked like a big white shoe box. It was old and crooked, with two sets of outdoor stairs and two wooden porches, upper and lower, that overlooked the Atlantic. Theirs was the last house on the block at the tip of the island, so the rest of Port Harbor—the tiny center of town, the hotels and the pizza shops and the boardwalk—seemed to be crowded to the north of us, on one side. Squinting against the sun, I looked up. A row of multicolored beach towels hung like flags from the railing on the second floor.

Ellen plucked a sheaf of letters from the mailbox. "Mostly bills," she said. "And junk mail." Raising her eyebrows, she tucked one letter into her purse, then whipped a rubber band from around her wrist and quickly fastened the others together.

"Thea! There you are. We've all been waiting for you," my Nenna said, opening her arms at the top of the steps as I walked up. She smelled of suntan lotion and ripe fruit. "Look: you're taller than I am," she said. "Granda, come and see who's here!"

Behind her, my Granda shuffled forward slowly. He was older than Nenna and very stiff; he had Parkinson's disease, which my dad said made it hard for him to move.

"Hi, Granda," I said. "How's it going?"

He moved his spotted hand toward me and made an awkward thumbs-up sign. He seemed a lot older than he had the year before.

"Come in! Do you want something to eat? Or drink?" Nenna asked. "What can I get for you?"

"We fed her, Mom," Ellen said. "We didn't abuse her or let her go hungry."

"Although we thought about it." Celia poked me in

19

the ribs with a sturdy finger. "Are you ready to face the crowd?"

Visiting my grandparents when my aunts and uncles and cousins were around was like walking headfirst into a storm. My father's relatives argued and interrupted each other in midsentence and shouted to each other from opposite corners of the house. I wasn't used to that kind of commotion. There might have been only eight people in Nenna's kitchen and living room, but it felt like eighteen.

"Hey, T! You're uglier than ever." My cousin Liam was eating ice cream from the carton in front of the open freezer, his mouth overflowing with vanilla fudge. My aunt Phoebe's baby, Ralph (I had almost forgotten he existed), was crying, the TV was on, Austin was yelling about someone having moved his binoculars, and my uncle Corey, Phoebe's husband, was on his way out the door with a set of golf clubs. He slapped me on the back. "Welcome to the madhouse." He laughed.

People hugged me and patted me and told me I'd grown. Outside the big sliding doors that led to the beach, the sun was flashing against the surface of the water. At the right time of day, I thought, the ocean looked like the world's largest broken mirror.

"It's a little noisy here," Nenna said. "Would you like to unpack?"

"Okay." I grabbed my bags and followed her up the stairs. We had to stick close to the wall to avoid my

Granda's mechanical chair. He could sit in it and press a button, and it would carry him all the way up the steps.

"One more flight." Nenna paused on the landing; she was out of breath. Her arms and legs were dark, her skin freckled and papery from more than half a century of summers spent in the sun. "I hope you won't be too warm up here," she said when we got to the attic. "I asked Ellen to get you a fan."

The attic wasn't as awful as it used to be. The rug was gone, and someone had cleared out a lot of the junk and pushed the boxes of old clothes and holiday decorations into a corner. Still, it wasn't a bedroom. It was more like a large hot open space, a sort of shapeless hallway at the top of the house. At one end, there was a tiny bathroom near the stairs. At the other end, near the window that overlooked the ocean, someone had set up two beds and two dressers.

"Jocelyn asked for the bed on the left," Nenna said, "which means this one's yours." She patted a metal army cot, the kind that looked like it would shriek every time I turned over.

"And let me see, where are your sheets? Here they are. It's so good to see you. There are plenty of towels in the downstairs closet. Will you want to go swimming right away?"

"No, thanks, Nenna."

"Maybe later, then."

"No, I don't think so." I looked at the blue-and-white-striped mattress. It was lumpy, and it made the bed look like a prisoner's. "I don't swim."

"Not at all?"

I shook my head.

Nenna cradled my face in her hands. "Oh, sweetheart," she said. "The world is not always gentle with us."

I asked her which dresser I should use.

"This one. I emptied the drawers for you."

"Thanks." I unzipped my suitcase. On top of a pile of shorts and T-shirts was a note from my parents. *Relax. Have fun. Remember that we love you,* the note said.

Nenna read it over my shoulder and said she thought that sounded like very good advice.

☆

The problem with the "have fun and relax" idea was that it wasn't easy to relax in a boxy old house with a dozen people, especially when at least half of them met my mother's definition of *eccentric*. There was the problem of dinner, for example. At home in Minneapolis, dinner was just my mother and my father and me. And even though my father had a few little quirks—he liked to line the silverware up beside the plates so that all the knives were facing the same direction—we usually managed to have a fairly normal meal.

Dinner in Port Harbor was a different story—not because it was noisy (which it was), but because of what my aunts and uncles called the dinner game. Even my father liked to play it. The dinner game surfaced whenever a lot of Grummans ate together.

"Oh, no," Austin groaned when he saw the folded strips of paper at each plate on the table. "Can't we just sit down and eat our food like regular people?"

"Blame your mother this time." Celia grinned. "She set up this round."

Nenna had made broiled flounder and baked potatoes and broccoli with cheese. Each of us was supposed to sit in front of the folded slip of paper that bore his or her name. As soon as the dishes were passed around, the guessing started.

"Is it height or weight?" Phoebe asked.

"No, too easy," Celia said. "Good flounder, Mom. Does Ralph count?"

"Only if he stays where he is."

The object of the game was to figure out what order we were sitting in. We might be seated according to age, or hair color, or the second letters of our middle names. Sometimes dinner was long over before anyone discovered what the answer was. I tried to distract myself by counting the ships on the faded wallpaper in front of me.

"What if we can't tell where Ralph's sitting?" Uncle Corey asked. "Is he to the right of Phoebe, or the left? Is there any butter?"

"Left," Ellen said. "Actually, I suppose it doesn't matter." Ralph was nursing, tucked up under Phoebe's shirt.

"Jeez, Phoebe," Austin said. "Do you have to do that at the table? I'm trying to eat dinner here."

"Don't be selfish," Phoebe told him. "You boys were both breast-fed. Weren't they, Ellen?"

"I'm going to pretend I didn't hear that," Austin said.

Twenty-eight, twenty-nine, thirty, thirty-one. I counted thirty-one wallpaper ships.

"What about shoe size?" Celia asked. She tapped her finger against her knife before picking it up. "Thea, pass the vegetables."

It seemed almost impossible to eat with the platters of food always circling.

"I don't like broccoli." Edmund scowled.

"No one likes broccoli." Austin ground so much pepper onto his potatoes, they almost turned gray. "Who invented this stupid game, anyhow?"

"No one remembers," Ellen said.

"That isn't true." Nenna raised her hand. "I invented it."

We all turned to stare at her.

"*You* did, Nenna?" Jocelyn asked. She was cutting her fish into itsy-bitsy perfect pieces.

Nenna put down her fork. "It was the only way I could think of to get my children to set the table. They used to fight for the opportunity," she said. "I didn't think they'd still be playing it when they were grown."

"Granda wants to say something," Liam announced.

My Granda had picked up his water glass as if getting ready to make a speech. But he just wiped a speck off the side of the glass and then drank from it. He winked.

"Maybe signs of the zodiac, alphabetically?" Uncle Corey asked. "Is there any more fish?"

"Nope. We did signs of the zodiac last year," Ellen said. "I remember because I'm the one who guessed it."

"Pass your Granda the bread and butter," Nenna said to Austin. "And don't read the sports page at the table. Thea, aren't you hungry?"

"I am," I said, "but I—"

"Middle names spelled backwards?" Phoebe asked. "Number of syllables in our names? Or number of letters?" She was burping Ralph against her shoulder.

"Ellen, will you tell us if we're getting closer?" Celia asked. "Does it have to do with our names?"

"Nope."

"Social Security numbers?"

"Nope."

I looked around the table, from Granda at one end, to Jocelyn and Edmund at the other. "It's the order we came here in," I said.

Everyone fell silent. Only Granda's fork continued to clink against his plate.

"Is that it?" Liam asked. "Is that the answer?"

I pointed at everyone around the table. "Nenna and Granda and Celia live here, so they're first. And then Liam and Austin, because they started working here in June, and then Edmund and Jocelyn, because they came a couple of days ago, and then Ellen and Phoebe and

Ralph and Corey. And I'm last—because I came today, and I'm here by myself."

"That sounds very lonely," Phoebe said. "I wouldn't exactly say that you're here by yourself."

"Of course you're not here by yourself," Nenna said. "And we're all very happy to see you."

"I'll eat that broccoli," Austin said. "If no one else wants it."

I passed him the broccoli. "I'm happy to be here," I said. I wasn't sure yet whether I was telling the truth or a lie.

CHAPTER FIVE

☆

It was only my second day in Port Harbor and already I had lost my mother's notebook. Maybe *lost* was the wrong word. I just hadn't come across it lately in any of the piles of clothes I was storing near the foot of my bed.

"What are you looking for?"

I turned around. My cousin Jocelyn had followed me up to the attic. She was like a miniature shadow. Whether I was reading or making a sandwich or just sitting in a rocking chair on the porch, Jocelyn would magically crop up beside me and ask me what I was doing.

Truth #4: It's not that I don't like little kids. I just shouldn't spend a lot of time with them. I really shouldn't be trusted.

"Nothing. I'm not looking for anything." I pawed through a mound of T-shirts spilling out of my suitcase.

"You *look* like you're looking for something. You're lifting things up and putting them down. And now you're pulling back the sheets on your bed. And you're lifting your pillow." Even though she was seven years old, Jocelyn looked about four. She and Edmund were both small for their ages, but Jocelyn was particularly tiny. Her hair was the largest thing about her: it was fluffy and yellow, like Easter grass. She had pulled it away from her face, but it frizzed and cascaded halfway down her back.

"I'm just moving things around." I shook the pillow (it had a moldy smell) out of its case. Where in the heck was that notebook?

"Aunt Ellen told me you would play a game with me," Jocelyn announced.

"Wasn't that nice of Aunt Ellen," I said, sitting down on the bed. The metal springs underneath me shrieked.

"We could play checkers. Or crazy eights or go fish. I'm good at go fish," Jocelyn said. "And I know how to shuffle."

"*I* know how to shuffle," said a second voice.

"No, you don't, Edmund," Jocelyn said. "You haven't learned."

"I don't want to play a game right now," I told her. "Maybe we could play later."

"Do you want to go swimming?" Like deer emerging from the woods, my cousins had crept a little closer. "I have my own raft this year," Jocelyn said, "but you can use it. Edmund and I aren't allowed in the water by ourselves."

"No, thanks. I don't want to go swimming." I dragged my backpack from under the bed.

"Why don't you want to go swimming?" Jocelyn asked.

The springs underneath me were chirping like crickets. "Because I just don't."

"Will you swim tomorrow?"

Truth #5: I really, really don't like sharing a bedroom.

"No," I said. "Probably not. I don't want to be out on the beach in the middle of the day. Because of the ozone. You know. The ozone layer is disappearing."

"Oh." Jocelyn straightened her headband. She was wearing green shorts and a green sleeveless shirt that looked like someone had recently ironed it.

I emptied my backpack onto the floor but found only CDs and books and half a peanut butter and jelly sandwich. Edmund was driving a filthy toy dump truck over my pillow. "Our parents are taking a vacation," he said. Edmund was so blond, he was almost white haired, with white eyebrows and lashes to match.

"They're in Europe," Jocelyn said, as if correcting him. "They're going to bring us some souvenirs."

"I think you might have told me that already," I said. About every twenty minutes Jocelyn needed to share another tidbit of information about her parents' trip. Her mother, my aunt Trisha, was leading a tour group through Italy and my uncle Gray had decided to go along. From Jocelyn I had recently learned that Italian pizza sometimes had fish on it, that the Pope wore a white gown and lived in Rome, and that even the little kids in Italy drank wine.

Edmund was grinning, driving his dump truck across my legs.

"Why haven't you put your clothes away?" Jocelyn peered down at the mess at my feet. "I could unpack for you. I'm good at unpacking."

I glanced at the surface of my cousin's dresser. It was perfectly, almost mathematically, arranged: a lamp, a clock, a brush and a comb, a white patent leather purse, and a pink jewelry box with a ballerina on its lid. There was even a little pink plastic dish with a collection of ponytail holders, evenly spaced, in a circle inside it. "No, but thanks anyway," I said.

"You shouldn't leave your clothes on the floor," Jocelyn told me. "If you do, you'll get fleas."

"Fleas?" Edmund's truck had left a scratch on my leg. "No one in this house has a cat or a dog."

"I'm talking about *sand* fleas," Jocelyn explained, as if she were a teacher instructing a particularly slow student. "I have to be careful about my skin because I have eczema. Eczema is a rash."

"I know what eczema is," I said. But because she

wanted me to, I examined the scaly pink patch on her forearm.

"Edmund, don't touch that," Jocelyn said. "That belongs to Thea."

Edmund had picked up the plastic case that held my toothbrush and toothpaste and shampoo and nail clippers.

"That's okay; he can look at it," I said.

Edmund promptly cut a hole in the bottom of my toothpaste tube with the clippers. He squeezed some paste out onto the floor.

"What's this?" Jocelyn asked. She had lifted the lid of my suitcase and found the notebook. "Is it your diary?"

"No." I snatched the notebook away from her. I fingered the white star on its cover. "I don't have a diary."

"Then what is it?"

"It isn't anything."

"Can I read it?"

"No." I stuffed the notebook under my pillow.

Edmund picked a scab off a mosquito bite and watched the blood trickle down to his ankle.

"I'm in the highest reading group at school," Jocelyn told me. "Ms. McGhee says I'm a very talented reader."

"I tasted my blood," Edmund said. "Look." He held up his finger.

"Don't you guys have something to do?" I asked.

"We want to play cards with you," Jocelyn said. "I brought the cards."

"Oh. Right." I put most of my clothes away in the

dresser, Jocelyn making suggestions about where I should keep my socks, and then we played go fish until Phoebe shouted for us to come downstairs.

Jocelyn stood up and brushed herself off: we'd been sitting on my bed—the dreaded sand fleas were probably everywhere. "Maybe we can sit next to each other at dinner," she said.

But Celia had seated us in alphabetical order of the cities we had been born in, so I sat between *L* for *Louisville* (my uncle Corey) and *P* for *Philadelphia* (Nenna). Phoebe accused Celia of cheating and Nenna had to tell them to behave themselves, but otherwise we had an uneventful meal.

☆

Truth #6: My parents are probably worried about me.

Truth #7: Sometimes I'm worried about myself.

Truth #8:

"Thea? Are you up there? Are you awake?"

Yes, I was awake. It was only eight-fifteen, but I'd been up for an hour. It was impossible to sleep late in the attic. There was no curtain on the window, and by the time the sun came blazing in, Jocelyn was rustling around like a little housewife, making her bed and getting dressed.

"Yoo-hoo!" It was Celia, shouting from the bottom of the stairs. "Thea? Hello! Are you there?"

Of course I was *there*. I was in the bathroom. It was the only place I could get any privacy. I opened the door about two inches and put my mouth and one eye into the opening. "What?"

"Can you come down here, please?"

"All right. One second." I shut the door again.

Truth #8:

"Thea? Can you hear me?"

I wanted to grind my teeth down to their roots. Four or five truths a day, my mother had said, as if they were vitamins. I clicked my pen.

"Thea?"

Truth #8: I wonder how many people my age have ever killed someone.

I stared at the notebook. "Coming," I said. But my feet appeared, momentarily, to be stuck to the floor.

Finally I managed to get out of the bathroom and stuff the notebook into a zippered compartment of my suitcase. Celia and Ellen were waiting for me. They stood at opposite sides of the kitchen, like two homely bookends.

"There you are," Celia said, as if I had been missing instead of shut in the bathroom two floors above her. "Ellen and I are off to work. Liam and Austin will be leaving soon, too."

"Okay." I opened the refrigerator and shook my head to clear my mind of the notebook. We didn't have any juice. Had Celia and Ellen brought me downstairs only to tell me they were going to work? "We need more orange juice," I said. "The kind without the pieces of orange in it."

Ellen took the silverware tray out of the dishwasher, sorted the knives and spoons (they were dirty, but that didn't stop her), and put it back in again. The backs of her legs were mapped with veins, a series of blue and purple threads beneath the skin.

I looked in the cabinets for a bowl and some cereal. All we had were bran flakes. I hated bran flakes. "We need more cereal, too," I said. "Maybe something with a little sugar in it?"

Liam and Austin sauntered into the kitchen, scratching themselves and smelling of sleep. They were like woolly animals emerging from a den. "I hate getting up in the morning," Austin said. "I'd rather not go to sleep at all. I'd rather just stay awake all night than have to get out of bed when it's still this early."

Liam found a stash of pancakes in the oven. He took one from the top of the stack, inserted it into his mouth like a funnel, and poured the syrup straight from the bottle down his throat.

"Can I have one of those?" I asked.

"You can make your own later," Austin said. "The important people have to go to work." He rolled his own pancake into a funnel. But Liam jabbed him in the stomach when he filled the funnel with syrup, and a sticky fountain erupted from Austin's mouth.

Ellen pointed a spatula at him. "Stop acting like savages," she said. She put three plates and three forks on the table, folded a napkin next to each, and said, "Sit." Liam and Austin and I all sat. Liam turned his plate around in a circle.

Celia looked at her watch. "You boys have exactly eleven minutes to eat and get dressed," she said. "And Thea, if you wouldn't mind, we've started some laundry you could finish while everyone's gone. Edmund had an accident last night; we're washing his sheets."

"Oh." I picked up my fork. Did I want to hear about people wetting their beds while I ate my breakfast? I looked out the sliding door to the porch. Edmund was talking to himself and mixing up something with a wooden spoon in a yellow bucket. Jocelyn was reading a book of fairy tales. Her headband matched her shirt and her socks.

"We decided that it would probably be a good idea," Ellen said, "for us to leave you a list in the morning, of any little chores that might need to be done. Things that you could take care of. By the way, the clothespins are in a plastic bag on top of the dryer. When you hang up the sheets, make sure you clip the pillowcases along the edges, not in the middle. If you hang them in the middle, they get a crease."

"I'll be sure to remember that." I put some butter on my pancakes. Did they actually expect me to start my day with a list of chores?

"Man, there's something sticky on me," Austin said.

35

He stripped off his shirt, turned it inside out, and then put it back on.

"Wait a second," I said. "Why do I need to hang up the sheets if we have a dryer?"

"We never dry sheets in the dryer," Ellen said.

"Why not?"

"Because we hang them outdoors." She picked up a purse so large she could probably carry a set of encyclopedias inside it. "I'm sure Jocelyn will be happy to help you. And you won't have to worry about Edmund, because we're dropping him off at Phoebe's."

I looked down at my pancakes. "What do you mean, I won't have to worry? Why would I worry about Edmund? Where's Nenna?"

"She's taking Granda to a doctor's appointment." Celia shut the refrigerator door with her hip. "They're leaving in half an hour."

Liam and Austin finished eating in about twelve seconds and went off to get dressed.

"So this is a one-time kind of thing," I said, measuring my words. "My watching Jocelyn, I mean. I'm going to babysit today because Granda has a checkup."

"That's today's schedule," Celia said.

"What about tomorrow's?" I asked. "I don't want to spend my vacation watching Jocelyn."

Ellen turned around. "Do you have any important plans in the next few days? Anything you won't be able to reschedule?"

"No, but—"

"Your Nenna is seventy-four years old," she said, leaning toward me. Her nostrils were as dark as caverns. "Do you want her to chase after a pair of kids while you eat potato chips and watch TV all day?"

"Do we have potato chips?" I asked.

We didn't.

Celia said she was sure it would all work out. She was sure I understood that a family vacation meant that every member of the family had to pitch in and help.

CHAPTER SIX

☆

**Truth #9: I don't think I would have come to
Port Harbor if I'd known that so many people
were going to be here.**

**Truth #10: But I didn't want to stay home,
either. Sometimes I wish I had the courage to
run away.**

"I'm okay by myself," Jocelyn said after everyone else
had left. "You don't have to pay any attention to me. I
know I'm supposed to leave you alone and not bother
you."

I put my notebook in the zippered pocket of my suitcase and stuffed the entire thing under my bed. "Who
told you not to bother me?"

"You did." She contemplated the objects on her
dresser, then moved her jewelry box half an inch to

the left. "Yesterday you told me I'm not supposed to follow you."

"Oh." I stood up and stretched, then looked in the mirror above my own dresser. My face was too round, I thought. Worse, my chin had a cleft in it, like a misplaced dimple. I had tried to flatten it out with masking tape once, but it hadn't worked.

"You're different this summer than you were last year," Jocelyn said.

"Am I?" I headed downstairs. "How am I different?"

"Your hair was longer last summer," Jocelyn said. She was following me again. "You let me braid it."

I remembered sitting on the living room floor watching some kind of movie while Jocelyn's fingers twined through my hair.

"And you were nicer," she added. "This summer you aren't as nice yet."

I turned around at the bottom of the steps. "Do you think I'll get nicer?"

Jocelyn scratched herself. "I have eczema on this arm now, too." She held her pale forearm up to the light, and I saw the peeling skin on her wrist and her hand, which was pink and rough.

I looked out the sliding door to the porch. The sun was hammering a silver path across the water. "I guess I'm supposed to do laundry now," I said. "If you want, you can help. But we have to do it Ellen's way, which means we're probably going to need a compass or a calculator." I opened the folding doors in front of the washing machine and dryer. Deep in the washer, Edmund's sheets were tangled up with socks and pajamas and a tablecloth and Granda's handkerchiefs. Old people used handkerchiefs, I had noticed. Why didn't they use tissues, like other people? I tugged at the heavy, soggy bundle. It was like trying to pull an octopus out of a hole.

"I saw you writing in your diary," Jocelyn said.

"It isn't a diary; I already told you." I dumped the laundry, including the balled-up sheets and a tiny pair of pajamas printed with elephants, into a plastic basket.

"Then what is it?" Jocelyn handed me a bag of clothespins. "Will you tell me what you wrote in it?"

"No."

"Why not?"

"Because I just won't. It's private. How often does Edmund wet his bed?"

"Not very often." She helped me carry the basket past the dryer (which looked almost new) and down the outdoor stairs. "I think at home it only happens a few times a week."

We set the basket down on the walk. The wind was blowing, and when I pulled the first sheet from the top of the pile, it flapped and clung to me, the cold cloth sticking to my legs.

"You haven't gone swimming yet." Jocelyn couldn't reach the clothesline, so she sat on one of the three wooden steps that led over the bulkhead to the beach. "You didn't go in the water yesterday or the day before. And you haven't gone in it today, either."

"Maybe I don't like swimming." I peeled the wet sheet off my legs and draped it over the line. By the time I pinned it into place, one long white edge was covered with sand. "Or maybe I went swimming before breakfast. Maybe I snuck out of the house and you didn't notice."

"There's no wet bathing suit on the clothesline," Jocelyn said. "And I would have noticed. Because I've been watching you."

"Why are you watching me?"

"Why aren't you going in the water?"

I pinned Edmund's pajamas and Granda's handkerchiefs to the clothesline. "I'm not going in the water because there are jellyfish," I said. The lie came to me easily, like a bubble rising up in a glass. "I'm allergic to jellyfish."

"Everyone's allergic," Jocelyn said. "Just like with bees."

"But I'm allergic in a different way," I said. "If I just put my toe in the water and there are jellyfish anywhere around, even ten feet away, my whole foot'll swell up and I won't be able to walk." I pinched my thumb with a clothespin. "It's called jell-itis."

Jocelyn studied me. "I never heard of that."

The sheets were flapping behind us in the breeze.

We didn't have anything else to do, so once I was finished with the laundry, I suggested that we walk to the

41

Ocean Market, a candy, magazine, and grocery store a few blocks down the beach. We went upstairs to get our sandals and some money. Jocelyn insisted on bringing her purse.

We climbed over the bulkhead and walked down the beach, past the lifeguard stand, which was bristling with signs that said, NO DOGS. NO PLAYING BALL. NO SWIMMING OUTSIDE THE GREEN FLAGS. NO TALKING TO GUARDS. The lifeguards both wore dark glasses. They stared at the water as if hypnotized.

"Do you think you'll ever show it to anyone?" Jocelyn asked.

"Show what to anyone?"

A man with a sunburned belly the size of a beach ball walked past us and tipped an imaginary hat.

"Your secret notebook," Jocelyn said. "Will you ever let anybody read it?"

"Let's talk about something else," I said. The sand was warm on top but cool underneath; I took off my flip-flops.

"You're not the only person here who's keeping a secret," Jocelyn said.

We saw a boy about Edmund's age sitting on a towel with a mountain of seaweed in a bucket beside him. He was popping the rubbery brown bubbles between his fingers.

"I guess you want me to ask you who has a secret," I said. "Okay—is it you?"

"No."

"Is it Nenna or Granda?"

"No. It's Aunt Celia and Aunt Ellen. I heard them whispering. They were in the kitchen and they didn't see me."

"They could have been whispering for a lot of reasons," I said. I remembered Ellen sifting through the mail, then tucking a single envelope into her purse. "Anyway, it isn't polite to eavesdrop."

"I'm good at eavesdropping," Jocelyn said.

We watched two girls in matching red bathing suits playing lacrosse at the edge of the water.

"Do you want to know what Aunt Celia and Aunt Ellen were whispering about?" Jocelyn asked.

"No."

The taller of the lacrosse-playing girls dropped the ball and had to run into the water to find it. I imagined the two of them going shopping together and seeing the bathing suits and deciding to buy them.

Jocelyn touched my arm. "Are you going to have friends here?"

"What do you mean?"

"I mean, if you have friends here, then you'll spend time with them. Edmund already has a friend named Brian. He lives next door."

When I was little—Jocelyn's age—I used to play in the sand with any other kids in Port Harbor who were building castles or digging holes or dragging water around in buckets. But I was too old for that now. "Maybe you'll have friends here," I said.

"No, I won't," Jocelyn said. "I don't have very many friends."

We left the beach, climbing the splintery stairs that led over the bulkhead. "Why don't you have very many friends?"

Jocelyn stopped to put on her sandals. She seemed determined to brush every single grain of sand from her feet. "Because I just don't."

Truth #11: I've never had very many friends, either.

"Some of the girls at school say I'm bossy," Jocelyn said.

"Are you bossy?"

"Kind of."

Truth #12: I used to have a best friend.

Truth #13: And her name was Gwen.

We had reached the street. Leaving the beach and going into the town of Port Harbor always felt strange to me. It was like opening a door and finding an entirely different world on the other side.

"Do you think you'll find out what the secret is— the one that Celia and Ellen are keeping?" Jocelyn asked.

"No." I shook a pebble out of one of my flip-flops. "I really doubt they're keeping secrets, Jocelyn."

We pushed through the door of the Ocean Market. The air was cold. It smelled like the inside of a cardboard box.

"Everyone always keeps secrets from me," Jocelyn said. "It's because I'm still young. If I was older, would you let me read what you've written in your diary?"

"No. And it isn't a diary. Do you want any candy? I'm getting something chocolate."

"I don't eat chocolate," Jocelyn said.

I chose two candy bars and a postcard and stood in line at the checkout counter.

Jocelyn tugged on my shirt. "But if Celia and Ellen *do* have a secret, and if you find out what it is, will you promise to tell me?"

Truth #14: I used to think secrets were kind of fun. But that was before I started lying to my parents, back in February.

"Will you, Thea?" Jocelyn scratched her arm. "Please? Thea?"

Because I thought she'd never drop the subject otherwise, I made her a promise. If I found out what the secret was, I would let her know.

CHAPTER SEVEN

☆

Most people think there are only two kinds of lies: "little white lies" and all the others. But that isn't true. Lies come in a lot of different colors.

White lies are the kind that protect other people's feelings. Yellow lies are the ones that tell only part of a story; they leave things out.

Then there are pink lies; the pink ones exaggerate.

Green ones invent. Little kids like to use them. ("I saw a dinosaur yesterday. It made a nest in my yard.")

Blue lies are the ones that people use when they're desperately trying to get out of trouble: "I didn't rob that bank. Really. I don't know where those bags of money came from."

And there are red and purple and orange lies. Gwen and I made the colors up. We sat down one day and wrote up a chart.

That was before I turned into a liar myself. And of course the first few lies I told were all about Gwen.

☆

It became pretty clear during the next few days that I was stuck with my little busybody cousin. It didn't matter whether I was on vacation or whether I said I didn't babysit. Liam and Austin were always at work (so were Celia and Ellen); Phoebe was busy with the baby (and had volunteered to entertain Edmund every morning, wearing him out so that he would take a nap every afternoon); and Nenna was usually cooking or doing some kind of housework. Besides, she had to help Granda. He needed help getting dressed and even getting in and out of his favorite chair.

Because Jocelyn was usually hovering somewhere nearby even when I wasn't officially spending time with her, the only moments I had to myself were at night in the attic. Sometimes I read under the covers with a flashlight. Or I took my notebook from the zippered compartment of my suitcase, chewed the cap of my pen, and waited to find out what I would write.

Truth #15: I have a lot of nightmares.

I glanced over at Jocelyn, a tiny lump on the opposite mattress.

Truth #16: I don't always remember them.
When I sit up in bed, the details disappear. It's

like shaking an Etch A Sketch: most of the picture gets rubbed away, so all you can see is an outline of what used to be there.

I sat in the dark and twirled my pen. Sometimes the truths came to me in bunches. Sometimes I thought of them during the day and had to carry them around with me for hours, until I had time to open my notebook.

Truth #17: I used to spend a lot of time at Three Mile Creek.

I paused; the pages of the notebook were smooth and thick.

Truth #18: I will never go to Three Mile Creek again.

"Thea?"

The notebook leapt out of my hands. "Jocelyn! You scared me to death. Why are you awake?" My heart was pounding.

"I heard you writing something." I could see the tangled fluff of her hair against the pillow. "You woke me up." She turned on the light. The only lamp in the attic was an old-fashioned one on Jocelyn's dresser. The bottom of the lamp was shaped like a lady wearing a giant hoopskirt.

"I couldn't have woken you up," I said. "I barely made any noise."

"I'm a very light sleeper." She rubbed her eyes and glanced at my notebook. "I have insomnia."

48

"Kids don't get insomnia." I put the notebook on my dresser, then thought better of it—hadn't Jocelyn told me she was in the highest reading group at school?—and stuffed it under my pillow.

"What were you writing about?" she asked.

"Nothing." I turned over and faced her. Our beds were parallel to each other, a six-foot stripe of floor between them.

"If I had a secret notebook, I'd write about all the things that other people hide from me. That's what I'd do. I'd write about secrets."

"You can turn the light out," I said. "I'm going to sleep."

She turned it out. "Why haven't you invited me to visit you in Minnesota?"

I could hear her scratching herself. She was always scratching. "I didn't know you wanted to come," I said.

"I do. If you invited me, I could go to school with you. And if it was winter, it would be cold outside and when we got home we'd drink hot chocolate with little marshmallows in it and play a duet on the piano."

"That's an interesting idea," I said, "except that I don't know how to play the piano. We don't even have one."

"You don't?" Jocelyn rustled around beneath her covers. "I thought everyone had a piano. Do you play the flute?"

"No."

"The clarinet?"

49

"I don't play an instrument."

It was quiet for several minutes. I thought Jocelyn might have gone to sleep. But then her voice floated toward me in the dark. "What do you do after school if you don't play an instrument? Do you play a sport?"

"No."

"Do you go to your friends' houses?"

I looked out the window. The night was a black box full of stars.

"Thea?"

"What?"

"Does it snow a lot in Minnesota?"

"Not in the summer," I said.

"Maybe when I visit you, we can go sledding," Jocelyn said. "It doesn't snow in New Jersey very often."

I closed my eyes. I didn't like thinking about the snow.

"Thea?"

"I'm tired, Jocelyn." As soon as she stopped talking, I thought, she would fall asleep. But I fell asleep instead. The next thing I knew, it was eight o'clock, and Jocelyn's bed was already empty, and very neatly made.

Dear Mom and Dad, It's sunny here. But it's not very hot. Everybody says hello. Love, Thea

Truth #19: I never know what to say on a postcard.

"Who are you writing to?" Jocelyn leaned over my shoulder. "Are your parents going to bring you a souvenir?"

"I doubt it," I said. "Unless they're planning to wrap up something from my bedroom and give it to me."

"My parents are bringing me something." Jocelyn picked up a pink marker and wrote, *This is from Jocelyn too*, on the bottom of my postcard. "But I can't write to them because I don't know where they are. All parents argue sometimes," she said.

"I guess so. Can I have my card back?"

Jocelyn was dotting the *i* in *this* with a little pink heart.

"Nenna, I'm going to the mailbox," I called. The house was quiet. Nenna and Granda and Jocelyn and I were the only ones home.

"What did you say, Thea?" Nenna wore hearing aids in both ears, but sometimes they didn't seem to work.

"I'm going out to mail a letter." When I turned around, Jocelyn was in front of the door, struggling with the buckles on her sandals. Across her chest she was wearing her patent leather purse.

"Where do you think *you're* going?" I asked.

"I'm going with you."

"Did you say you're going to the store, Thea?" Nenna had taken the hearing aid out of one ear. She tapped it against the back of her hand. "Would you mind picking up a gallon of milk?"

51

"I'll do it, Nenna," Jocelyn said, raising her hand as if she were in school. "I'm going with Thea."

"Good girl." Nenna gave her a kiss. Then she kissed me, too. She tucked several bills into Jocelyn's purse.

We bought the milk and a pack of gum (Jocelyn insisted that we buy sugarless), and I mailed my postcard on the way back. *Hello, Minneapolis.* It was ten in the morning. I figured I had seven more hours to kill until someone else might be interested in taking charge of my cousin.

"Aunt Celia said you would take me swimming today," Jocelyn said. She lifted her hair—it was more like a scarf—off the back of her neck.

"Aunt Celia must have been confused about that," I told her.

We delivered the milk to Nenna and went back outside.

"If I go down to the water and look for jellyfish and make sure there aren't any, then will you go swimming?"

"No," I said.

"But Aunt Celia said you would take me. We're at the *beach*."

"I *know* where we are."

Jocelyn looked disappointed.

"All right, listen." I didn't want her tattling to Celia and Ellen, in case there was any chance of my getting paid. "If you'll stop asking me about going swimming, I'll tell you one thing—*just one*—about my notebook. But then you have to stop nagging me. All right?"

Jocelyn considered the rash on her arm. She seemed to be thinking. "All right."

"Okay, then." The wind changed direction and the air felt cooler all of a sudden, as if someone had opened a giant window.

"So what is it?" Jocelyn asked. "What are you going to tell me?"

What *was* I going to tell her? I took a deep breath. "Well, this isn't something that I've written down, but it's about the notebook. I'm using it to write down things that are true. True things that matter. So it isn't a diary. It's just a bunch of, you know, a bunch of true things."

"So it's a list," Jocelyn whispered, as if I had revealed to her the secrets of the ancient pharaohs. "What kind of true things are they? How many pages do you have so far?"

I didn't appreciate the way her mind worked. "I said *one thing. One.* Now, let's look around for something to do."

Jocelyn skipped behind me, suddenly cheerful, as we went around the outdoor stairs to the storage area, a musty cinder-block garage at the front of the house. It was stacked from cement floor to ceiling with broken beach chairs and rusted umbrellas and a rotting volley-ball net and horseshoes and fishing poles. There was a metal shelf full of paint cans and batteries. Celia hated to throw anything out.

"Okay," I said, looking at the piles of cobwebbed stuff. "Do you want to play horseshoes?"

"No. They're all rusty."

"What's this problem you have with dirt and bugs and rust? Should we play croquet?"

"No. There isn't enough grass here," she pointed out.

I pushed a toolbox and a stack of apple crates out of the way.

"I know what you should write about in your notebook," Jocelyn said. "You should write down everything we find out about Aunt Celia and Aunt Ellen's secret."

"They don't have a secret, Jocelyn," I said.

"Yes, they do. They drive to work together."

I stubbed my toe on the toolbox. "So?"

"They work in opposite directions," Jocelyn said. "Aunt Ellen doesn't even work in Port Harbor."

I turned around. She was right. Ellen spent the night at her own house, ten miles away, but came to Nenna and Granda's every morning for breakfast. "She probably just wants to see Liam and Austin," I explained.

"Look, there's an inner tube." Jocelyn pointed. "We can blow it up with the pump and take it in the—oh." She looked at me sideways.

"That tube probably has a hole in it, anyway," I said. "I know what we can do." I nudged a path through the wreckage. "Do you know what the great thing about Port Harbor is?"

"No, what?"

"It's small," I said, "which means you can get anywhere on a bike. And this one—*oof!*—right here should be short enough for you." I lifted the volleyball net and revealed a pink bike with a banana seat and moldy streamers dangling from the handlebars. "I used to ride this. It's great. I can clean it for you. Help me get it outside."

Jocelyn didn't budge.

"Come on. What's the matter? It'll be fun."

"I don't know how to ride a bike," she said.

Several streamers fell to the floor of the garage. "You don't know how? You're seven, and you can't ride a bike?"

She folded down her ankle socks, aligning them perfectly along her skinny calves. I was desperate to go somewhere, to get away from the house and the list of chores Ellen had probably left on the refrigerator. (*Thea: Replace engine in car. Pour cement for driveway. Reroof garage.*) "We could ride double on one bike," I said, glancing at the dark green model I'd been planning to ride.

"Riding double isn't safe," Jocelyn said.

Muttering darkly to myself, I shoved the pink bike back into place, then waded deeper into the garage. I pushed past the charcoal grill and the rusted lawn mower and the coils of garden hose that reminded me of bright green snakes, and then, in the corner, I discovered something I had almost forgotten: the giant trike.

"I think that's Granda's," Jocelyn said.

It was. I squeezed the hand brake on the oversized three-wheeler and remembered that when I was little, my Granda used to put me in the rectangular wicker basket in front of him and pedal me around Port Harbor. He used to sing, too. He sang songs from old movies, from *Oklahoma!* and *South Pacific*. He had a soft, deep voice— the kind you could feel inside your chest. He probably couldn't pedal the trike anymore. And I hadn't heard him sing in years.

I shoved the grill and the hose out of the way and dragged the trike into the sunlight. "I bet you'd fit in that basket," I said. I found a bike pump and started pumping up the tires. I plucked some spiders' eggs from the spokes.

Jocelyn looked skeptical.

"Look," I said. "We can sit here dusting and doing laundry all day, or we can go exploring. Which sounds more interesting to you?"

I helped her climb up. Her thighs weren't much bigger than my wrists and easily slipped through the wicker openings. "We aren't going very far, are we?" she asked.

"We're on an island." I pushed the trike onto the sidewalk. "There isn't very far to go."

"Thea, wait. I don't have a seat belt."

A seat belt? I found a yellow bungee cord hanging on a peg by the garage door. "Here. This'll be perfect. Some people even use them in cars, they're so safe."

"Really? Do they?"

"Sure. Would I lie to you?"

Jocelyn fastened the bungee to the wicker basket, stretching it like a belt across her waist.

"Are you ready?" I asked.

She straightened her headband and nodded. "Let's ride."

CHAPTER EIGHT

☆

Port Harbor was small, and there was almost no traffic. As soon as we rode away from the house, I began to feel free, like a dog whose owner had unfastened its leash and let it run.

"What are we going to explore?" Jocelyn shouted. She looked like a statue on the front of an old-fashioned ship.

I was pedaling too hard to answer. I had to stand up because the trike was heavy. Wiry yellow strands of Jocelyn's hair kept floating or blowing into my mouth.

"We're going past the museum," Jocelyn announced, like a miniature tour guide. "And there's the fish store." She pointed at a peeling wooden sign: LANDVIK'S FRESH FISH. "I went there with Nenna."

I plopped down behind her on the vinyl seat. We rode past the Port Harbor Fire and Rescue, past the

Knitting Niche, the Seaway Hotel, and Francisco's Pizza. I turned right and headed into the breeze. "Can you tell where I'm taking us?" I asked.

"No." Jocelyn's legs were dangling on either side of the wide front tire like pale white fruit.

About eight blocks later, we glided to a stop.

"Look over there," I said. "See the ramp? We made it all the way to the boardwalk." About twenty-five yards ahead of us was a mile-long stretch of rides and bumper cars, fun houses, spin-paint booths, Skee-Ball, cotton candy, caramel corn, and a Ferris wheel with colored compartments that swayed and revolved above the ocean. "Get out and help me push," I said.

Jocelyn scratched her arm. "I'm not allowed to go to the boardwalk."

I could smell the pizza, the fudge, the cheesesteaks frying on a dozen grills. "You're not *allowed*?" I asked. "Why not?"

She tried to turn around in her seat, but the yellow bungee cord held her in place. "They only sell junk food up there. I don't eat junk food. Besides, there are pickpockets. And people who try to steal your money."

"Pickpockets?" My legs felt like rubber. I got off the trike and moved aside for a woman with a stroller. "Do you have any diamond rings with you?"

"No."

"Do you think someone is going to force you to eat a bag of candy?"

Jocelyn shook her head, then pushed her nest of yellow hair behind her ears. "I can only come here with an *adult*," she said. "That's the rule."

"I'm twelve and a half," I pointed out.

Up ahead I could see a juggler on a unicycle, and a mime with a white-painted face holding an oversized bouquet of helium balloons. I loved the boardwalk, even the parts of it I was too old for. I loved the smell of salt water and frying food, the *pit-a-ping* of the pinball machines, and the hollow thump of the boards beneath my feet. I looked at my cousin. I already knew she had a price. "I'll tell you one more thing about my notebook."

She licked her lips. "Two things."

"Don't be greedy." I started pushing the trike up the ramp. "Okay. I'm going to write one hundred things in it," I said. "Exactly one hundred."

"Why exactly one hundred?"

We reached the top of the ramp. "Because when I get to a hundred . . ." I was searching for words. "Then the book will be finished."

"And then what? Will you let people read it?"

"No. But I might discover something," I said.

"What will you discover?"

"I don't know yet." I climbed back on the trike. We rode past the haunted house, the taffy-pulling machine, the tattoo parlor, the photo booth, the house of mirrors, half a dozen small shops, and the arcades. Finally I coasted to a stop in the shade of a bandstand.

Jocelyn struggled to turn around. "Why are we stopping?"

"Because it's hot up here," I said. "And my legs are tired."

Just ahead of us, a boy was throwing pizza crust to a crowd of seagulls. Their squeaky cries and complaints filled the air.

"I can't believe I pedaled us all the way here and didn't bring any money," I said. "I'm going to die of thirst."

A man dressed as a giant hamburger waddled toward us, hand in hand with a woman dressed as a cup of french fries.

I accepted a coupon from the human hamburger: *75 cents off any large sandwich!*

"What's that?" Jocelyn asked. In one of the arcades across from us, two girls in shorts and bathing suit tops were dancing on a metal platform that boomed out music, a series of colored lights and arrows telling them where to move their feet.

"It's a kind of game," I said. "I guess it's supposed to teach you how to dance."

"Is it fun?"

"I don't know. I've never tried it."

The dancing girls bent their knees and swayed their hips. Five feet away from them, a woman in a uniform came out of the fudge shop with a tray of free samples, little cubes of bliss.

"Don't your parents ever bring you here?" I asked. "You only live about an hour away."

"My father doesn't like the boardwalk," Jocelyn said. "But sometimes we come in the fall. When it isn't crowded."

"Most of the boardwalk is closed in the fall," I pointed out.

The boy who had been feeding his pizza crust to the seagulls was staring at our trike. He threw a final piece of crust and a bird caught it neatly in midair, then sailed away over the ocean.

"What's that?" Jocelyn asked.

I shaded my eyes and tried to figure out what she was looking at. I saw a store selling hermit crabs, a rolling cotton candy booth, and a lemonade stand. I was desperately thirsty. I tried not to think about the ice and the juicy lemons, about the soggy swirls of sugar at the bottom of the cup. "Are you asking about the hermit crabs?"

"No. I'm asking about *her*."

Between a frozen custard booth and the turbaned man who advertised YOUR NAME PAINTED ON A GRAIN OF RICE was a fortune-teller. She was sitting at a table in a narrow doorway, filing her nails. Over her head was a sign made of tiny plastic silver coins that trembled in the breeze. The shiny letters spelled KNOW YOUR FUTURE.

"Oh. I guess she's a fortune-teller," I said. "You give her five dollars and she looks at your hand, or at a crystal ball or something." A smaller sign hanging from the edge of the table promised that Madam Carla Knows.

62

"Then what does she do?" Jocelyn asked.

"She probably tells you your fortune—you know, what's going to happen to you. You probably ask her a bunch of questions and she answers them."

"What do you usually ask her?"

"What?" I was still daydreaming about sugar and lemons. "I don't ask her anything. I've never gone to her."

"What would you ask her for if you *did* go?"

The fortune-teller had put her nail file away; she seemed to be gazing toward us. "She isn't like Santa Claus," I said. "You don't ask her for stuff and wait for her to hand it over. You ask about the future. She's supposed to know things about you."

Jocelyn looked almost frightened. "I know what I'd ask her for," she said.

A bell rang behind us. Two men on a double bike pedaled by. They were followed by a woman pushing an ice cream cart, a silver refrigerator on wheels. I wondered aloud if the woman might take pity on us and give us some water.

"Do you want me to buy you something?" she opened her patent leather purse.

I stared at her. "You've got money?"

"It's the change from the milk." She climbed gracefully out of the basket.

"That's Nenna's money," I said. "But I guess she wouldn't mind if we used it."

The ice cream woman paused beside us. "Can I get you two ladies something?" Her voice was gravelly and low, and she had a mole on her face that was shaped like a comma.

"Do you have sherbet or Popsicles?" Jocelyn asked.

"You don't want an ice cream?" I studied the pictures on the side of the cart.

"Ice cream is high-fat," Jocelyn said.

I looked her up and down. Some of the Grummans—Celia and Ellen, in particular—had what my mother called generous figures. I liked to consider myself medium-sized. But Jocelyn was a waif. She probably weighed about forty pounds.

"Besides, I'm allergic to dairy foods," she added. "They're not good for my skin. I always have to be careful."

"You *are* always careful," I said.

The ice cream woman turned her head and bellowed as if she were in pain: *"EEEEiiiiice creeeeeam! Get your ice-cold-eeeeeice-cream heeeeere!"*

Jocelyn bought two medium lemon ices, tucking the change back into her purse, and we sat on a bench with our backs to the ocean. We peeled away the sticky paper lids and licked them. "I think we should go exploring like this every day," she said, chopping her lemon ice with a wooden spoon. "We'll borrow Granda's trike and we'll ride everywhere in Port Harbor. And we won't tell anyone where we're going."

Truth #20: Not telling anyone where you're going is incredibly stupid.

64

I took a huge bite of lemon ice and let it melt against the roof of my mouth. "We should have left a note," I said. "We should have left a note for Nenna." I took another bite of lemon ice, then pinched the bridge of my nose with my fingers. The space behind my eyes was tingling: I was getting a brain freeze. "Ow." I leaned forward on the bench. The brain freeze was creeping up into my sinuses, making me feel as if someone were ramming a pair of icicles up my nose. "Ow, ow, ow." I pushed my fingers into my eye sockets.

"You ate too fast," Jocelyn said. "Don't poke your eyes. I know what to do." She quickly stood up, put down her lemon ice, and pressed her fingertips against my temples and the bridge of my nose. Then she squeezed my head gently, smoothing my eyebrows with her thumbs.

The icicles in my nostrils were gradually melting. "Thanks," I said. "How'd you learn to do that?"

"Close your eyes," Jocelyn said.

I did. But then I remembered the peeling skin on her hand and I needed to see if it was touching my forehead. Was eczema contagious? Imagining my face looking like an iguana's, I opened my eyes. Over Jocelyn's shoulder, I saw someone who looked almost familiar: a middle-aged woman clutching an oversized purse.

"That's weird," I said, nudging Jocelyn aside. "That woman over there almost looks like Aunt Ellen."

Jocelyn sat down beside me on the bench, our legs touching. The woman, dressed in a tan knee-length skirt and a flowered T-shirt—wasn't that what Ellen had been wearing when she left the house?—looked at her watch and waved to someone. It had to be Ellen, I thought. I recognized the muscular legs beneath the hem of her skirt.

"What are they doing up here?" Jocelyn shaded her eyes.

"They?" I asked. And then I saw Celia walk toward Ellen. Our aunts stood in the sun and seemed to be arguing. Nothing new there. Ellen held out her hand and Celia dropped something into it. Something small. It glinted in the sun for half a second, and then Ellen tucked it into her purse.

"Aren't they supposed to be at work?" Jocelyn asked. "Do you think they're looking for us?"

"No. They couldn't be. They don't know we're here."

We watched Celia and Ellen walk away, still arguing, a crowd of people in shorts and T-shirts eventually blocking them from sight.

Jocelyn opened and closed her little purse, playing with the clasp. Open-snap, open-snap. Her lemon ice had turned into a puddle. "Now you'll believe me," she said. "Now you'll believe there really is a secret."

"I don't believe anything," I told her. But I had a strange feeling in my stomach, as if I had swallowed a large ball of cotton.

Open-snap. Open. "Here, do you need this? We can share it." Jocelyn offered me a folded wet cloth in a paper pouch.

"A hand wipe?" I was amazed. "You actually carry these around with you?"

Jocelyn took the wipe out of its little square pouch and ripped it in half. "Are your hands sticky?"

They were. I took my half and wiped my hands and face.

We sat on our wooden bench in the sun, the ocean a blue and gray murmur behind us.

"I think you should write this down in your notebook," Jocelyn said.

"That's not what my notebook is for," I told her. I tossed my lemon ice into the trash.

Truth #21: Maybe Ellen and Celia are up to something after all.

CHAPTER NINE

☆

To avoid Jocelyn's questions for a little while, I volunteered for salad duty that afternoon, which meant I had to spend an hour at the kitchen sink, washing heads of lettuce and getting the little black bugs out of their wrinkled leaves. Then I had to peel and chop what seemed like a zillion carrots and radishes and tomatoes.

Ellen came clattering toward me, carrying a tray full of dirty dishes. "Are you cutting those radishes into quarters?"

I looked at the cutting board. "I guess."

"Slices are better." She started filling the sink with soapy water. Everyone was wandering into the kitchen, looking for a snack or a preview of dinner.

"I always cut radishes into shapes," Phoebe said, swaying by with Ralph. "You know, like flowers."

"Flowers?" I stared at the little red globes under my

knife. She might as well have told me to carve them into statues of movies stars and famous athletes.

"It doesn't matter to me, though," Phoebe said. "I'm not going to eat them. They aren't good for Ralph." She bounced the baby on her hip. "I think they make my milk taste funny. Or maybe—"

"Please," I said. I dumped the radishes into a bowl and went on to the carrots. Ellen insisted that they be *grated* instead of chopped.

"Did anyone get their Granda his beer?" Nenna asked. Every afternoon, my Granda drank a single small glass of beer. When I was younger, I sometimes used to take it to him out on the porch, and after he sipped from the frosted glass we would both laugh at the foamy mustache on his lip.

"I'll get it," Celia said. "Whoops. Shove over, Thea."

I took a step to the left but didn't look up. I was concentrating on the grater. The last time I had used it, I'd torn off a piece of my index finger.

"Man, I think I made about a thousand and one steak sandwiches today," Liam said, taking a seat at the counter. "You wouldn't believe the amount of grease we scrape off that grill. It's truly disgusting."

"How was everyone else's day?" Nenna asked.

"Ours was fine," Phoebe said. "Ralph and I had a little nap. Didn't we, Ralphums?"

Nenna kissed my newest cousin's pale bald head. "What about you, Thea?"

"What? My day? Oh, it was fine." I swept the orange mound of vegetables into the salad. "Jocelyn and I just hung around. We went for a walk. We ate some lemon ice. You know." (A yellow lie. I wasn't making anything up, but I was leaving things out.)

Edmund started yelling about a water-skier who was doing tricks, and everyone turned to the window to look.

"What did everybody else do?" I asked. I arranged the radishes in a little circle around the salad.

"Went to work," Ellen said.

Celia had poured Granda's beer and delivered it. "Went to work is right." She sat down next to Liam. "We've got an orthodontics convention at the hotel this week. It turns out that orthodontists don't like muffins with their breakfast. They only like toast. And they don't like the shower mats in their bathrooms. I had to call a meeting about those mats. I was in and out of meetings all afternoon."

I looked up from the salad—now a masterpiece of lettuce and vegetables—and spotted Jocelyn standing in the doorway. "What about in the morning?" I asked.

"What do you mean?" Celia scooped one of Ralph's plastic chew toys off the floor.

"I just wondered." I put the cutting board next to the sink. "You know—whether you were stuck in meetings in the morning, too. Because it was nice out. So I just wondered if you spent the entire day indoors."

There was a pause, like a quarter rest in a piece of

music. "Unfortunately," Celia said, "when you're the manager of a hotel, you work indoors."

An orange lie—she hadn't answered my question.

I poured myself a glass of water and added a slice of lemon to it. The water in Port Harbor always tasted like metal.

"I think dinner's ready," Ellen announced.

Jocelyn stood quietly in the doorway, scratching her arm.

☆

Truth #22: Temperatures in Minnesota have ranged from –60, in the winter, to 114. The first freeze usually comes in October, and the last one can come as late as May. Maybe those are facts instead of truths. I had to use Nenna's encyclopedia to look them up.

"She was lying. Aunt Celia lied to us—you heard her." It was ten-fifteen. Why wasn't Jocelyn asleep? Weren't people her age supposed to sleep? But she had obviously been waiting up for me in the attic, the lady-in-a-hoopskirt lamp shining its yellow light on her pillow.

"She might have forgotten what she did today," I said. "Maybe she got mixed up."

"No. She was lying," Jocelyn insisted. "Because she knew you were asking about the secret."

"Whatever." There was no use explaining to Jocelyn about all the different kinds of lies. And I had plenty of things to think about other than Celia and Ellen and their trip to the boardwalk. I turned out the light, then lifted my pillow, found my pajamas, and put them on.

Jocelyn's voice floated toward me. "Do you think you'll have nightmares tonight?"

"What do you mean? How do you know I have nightmares?"

"Because I can hear you. You kick off your covers and flop around. And you talk in your sleep sometimes. Will you tuck in my covers?"

I gave her blanket a quick yank. "What do I talk about? In my sleep?"

Jocelyn fluffed up her pillow. "Tighter," she said. "They have to be really, really tight. Or else I can't sleep. I have insomnia."

She was going to drive me insane. I walked around her bed, pulling and tucking the sheet and the blanket as tightly as I could. When I was finished, she looked like a letter in an envelope. I climbed into bed.

"Thea?"

"What?"

"Do you ever babysit in Minnesota?"

Truth #23: I used to babysit.

"No," I said.

"Why not?"

"I just don't like to."

"Oh." Jocelyn yawned. "I know where you're keeping your notebook," she said.

I sat up. "Have you looked at my notebook?"

"No. But you should probably hide it somewhere else. It makes a bump in your suitcase."

I lay back down. "I shouldn't have to hide it, Jocelyn," I said. "You should promise not to read it."

"Promises are hard," Jocelyn said. "People break promises all the time." Through the window at our feet, the moon was a perfect coin above the water. "Can we ride the trike tomorrow?" she asked.

I told her we could.

"And you'll tell me one more thing about your notebook," she said. "And then we'll spy on Aunt Celia and Aunt Ellen."

I yawned. "People don't like to be spied on," I said.

"If they don't know you're spying, then it doesn't bother them." Jocelyn struggled to turn toward me, her shoulders pinned beneath the sheet. A minute later I could hear her scratching.

"Maybe you should leave that rash alone for a while," I said. "Wasn't Nenna going to buy you a new kind of cream?"

"She already did." More scratching. "But I don't like the smell of it. Thea?"

"What?" I straightened my pillow.

"How do you always know the answer to the dinner game?"

"I don't always know it. I guess it seemed obvious tonight." Phoebe had arranged us in order of appetite, with Austin first. I had glanced around the table and seen Austin and Liam shoveling food into their mouths; then everyone else at the table simply fell into place.

"I didn't think it was obvious," Jocelyn said. "You could probably guess anything. Because you're smart. And you figure things out."

"Good night, Jocelyn." I heard a click from the downstairs hallway: someone was turning out the lights. A door closed below us, and the stairs that led to the attic disappeared in the dark.

CHAPTER TEN

☆

I woke up the next morning because someone was poking me with a finger. "I want to draw a dinosaur," Edmund said. "But I don't know how."

I could feel a dream hovering, just out of reach. In the dream, Celia was marrying Mr. Hanover. One of her bridesmaids was a fish, and it wore a long green dress with a matching veil. "I love your outfit," I told the fish.

Edmund poked me again, and I pulled up an eyelid. Jocelyn's bed was already made. I felt as if someone had roughed up my brain with a piece of sandpaper. "Draw something easier," I told Edmund. "Draw a bird. Or a stick." I tried to roll over. Sleep was still waiting for me, like my own dark cocoon.

"I don't want to draw a *stick*." Edmund tugged my covers. "I want to make a birthday card for Nenna."

Some of my hair was stuck to my cheek. I peeled it away and sat up, remembering my conversation with Jocelyn from the night before. It was time to hide my notebook.

I looked at Edmund. "It isn't anyone's birthday today," I said. "Nenna's birthday is in January."

This didn't seem to bother him. He still wanted to make her a birthday card. "I have my markers," he said. "Look." He held a green felt-tip marker about half an inch away from my nose.

"All right, all right. Just give me a minūte." I scanned the attic for a hiding place. I couldn't hide the notebook in my bed. Even when I made the bed (normally I didn't), Jocelyn insisted on correcting my work by smoothing out the wrinkles. I couldn't hide it in my dresser, either— that was probably the first place Little Miss Curious-Pants would look. Until I could come up with something better, I decided to settle for a box of winter clothes in the corner—and a booby trap. That was an old trick that Gwen had taught me. I put two human hairs and ten grains of sand on the notebook's first page. If anyone picked up the notebook or tried to read it, the hair and the sand would all fall out.

Truth #24: Gwen and I used to hide things from her little sister.

"Okay, Edmund, I'm ready." I managed to help him draw a green stegosaurus that looked like a dog. A bubble coming out of its mouth said, *Happy Big Dinosaur Birthday to Nenna*.

"There," I said. "What made you think it's Nenna's birthday, anyway?"

"Aunt Ellen said it was." Edmund held up the drawing with both hands so that he could admire it.

"Ellen did? I kind of doubt that, Edmund." I rubbed the sleep from my eyes and brushed my hair.

"She did," he insisted. "She said it wasn't a very good surprise for Nenna, because she's getting old."

I put down my hairbrush. "What isn't a very good surprise?"

"I don't know."

"Well, who was Ellen talking to?"

"I don't know," he said again. "She was on the phone."

I went into the bathroom to get dressed while Edmund waited, and then I carried his markers and his pad of paper down the two flights of stairs to the kitchen. Nenna was pouring herself a cup of coffee. She hadn't gotten dressed yet; she was wearing her blue flowered bathrobe and matching slippers. On anyone else, an outfit like that would have looked ridiculous. On Nenna, I thought, it was graceful and pretty.

"Hey, Nenna," I said.

"Good morning, Thea."

Edmund bounded toward her and pushed his face into her stomach.

"There you are!" she said, rubbing his hair. "I had a dream about you last night. I woke up and thought, *There's Edmund. In the morning I'll be able to see him outside my dream.*" She listened to him ramble on about his picture, which they taped to the refrigerator door.

Truth #25: My Nenna is probably the kindest and most patient person on the face of the planet.

The kitchen was empty. "Where is everyone?" I asked.

She sipped her coffee. "Liam and Austin are still asleep. They have the day off." She tickled the back of Edmund's neck. "Phoebe was here, but she just left. She put the baby down for an early nap and went out for a walk. And your Granda is resting."

My Granda used to be the first one up in the morning. He used to open the porch door and the windows and say, "Look what the day's going to bring us!"

I looked past the counter with its row of mismatched vinyl stools; the living room was empty, too. "What about Jocelyn?"

"She's out with Celia. They're running some errands. We needed more soap for the kitchen, and there's a particular kind that Ellen likes to use. I think it comes in a yellow bottle."

Only Ellen would care about a particular kind of dish soap.

"But she left you a note," Nenna said. "Jocelyn did,

that is. Where did I put it? I understand it's highly confidential." She handed me a piece of paper that was folded up into a square and taped shut on the edges. On the outside it said, *For Thea Only. Only Thea Can Reed This.*

I slit the tape with my fingernail and unfolded the page. It was pink, with a row of kittens across the top. *I am folowing her,* the note said. *I will be bak.*

I refolded the note, dropped it into the trash, and looked around the kitchen for something to eat. "Half the people in this house have gone bonkers," I muttered.

"I'm sorry, Thea?" Nenna took out her hearing aid and tapped it against the kitchen counter. "Sometimes they make a whistling noise." She fit the device back inside her ear. "Edmund, would you lower the sound on the TV, please?"

Edmund had parked himself in front of some kind of nature show: a snake about twenty feet long was eating something, and the back half of the something was still kicking and squirming.

"There. That's better. What were you saying, Thea?"

"Nothing. I was just saying that, you know, sometimes it seems like Celia and Ellen are . . ." I remembered my mother's word. ". . . eccentric. And Jocelyn's kind of that way, too."

Nenna took a broom from the hall closet. "I've been meaning to tell you," she said, "it's very sweet of you to spend so much time with Jocelyn. I can tell she looks up to you."

I found a banana in a bowl on the counter. It had some brown spots on one side, so I put it back. "I doubt she looks up to me," I said. "I haven't been all that nice to her."

Truth #26: Theodora Grumman is not a nice person. A nice person would not have done the things I did at Three Mile Creek.

"I'm sure that's not true," Nenna said. "You've been very generous and accommodating, agreeing to share a room this year. And I think it does Jocelyn a lot of good. Personally, by the way, I've always found you very impressive."

My Nenna was four inches shorter than I was, but I wanted to put my head on her shoulder. Or even sit on her lap. "What do you mean, you think it does her a lot of good?"

"I'm sorry?"

I tried to speak up. "What's the deal with that rash of hers?" I asked. "It looks like it's spreading."

"I wouldn't worry about the rash," Nenna said. "It's not contagious. Most people grow out of it. Would you get me that dustpan, please? Of course, anxiety and stress can make eczema worse."

I handed her the dustpan. "But Jocelyn doesn't have anything to be stressed out about."

The giant snake on TV (was it the same snake or a different one?) was laying a cluster of wet, leathery eggs in a little burrow.

"I'm sure everyone has their own roster of difficulties," Nenna said. She opened the sliding door and together we stepped out onto the porch, where the sun was still burning off a layer of morning fog. My Nenna swept the sand off the porch every morning, and by afternoon it was covered with sand again. She was always moving, always busy. She seemed to have a list of things to do that revolved in her head.

"I doubt Jocelyn has very many difficulties," I said.

Nenna nudged a small pile of sand off the edge of the porch.

"If she does, she probably invented them herself. She's always scheming and fussing with things," I said, sitting down. "And rearranging the stuff on her dresser."

Nenna collected some newspapers that someone had strewn across the wicker sofa. "I remember when you were Edmund's age you discovered counting," she said. "You counted everything. The number of steps on the staircase, the number of forks in the silverware drawer. You wanted everything to come out even."

"That was different." I blushed. "I was five years old." I lifted my feet so that she could sweep in front of me. "Are you saying that I'm as weird as Jocelyn?"

Nenna leaned her broom against the wall. "No. I'm saying there's nothing wrong with counting. Or rearranging your dresser. Grummans tend to be creatures of habit."

I pictured Ellen and Phoebe and Celia and Nenna and Granda and Jocelyn and even Liam and Austin as Creatures, with rubbery skin and tentacles and hooves.

Truth #27: I don't want to be a Creature of Habit.

I remembered an afternoon when Mr. Hanover, the school counselor, had paused in the middle of a sentence because he had been watching me touch each of my fingertips to my thumbs, back and forth, from my index fingers to my pinkies. It kept my hands busy, and I was nervous. Mr. Hanover had leaned toward me, his gleaming black shoes sliding under his chair along the carpet, and said, "Thea? That little mannerism with your fingers? Is that something you *have* to do?"

Nenna tucked the newspapers under her arm, picked up her broom, and opened the screen door. I followed her. What if I *was* as weird as Jocelyn? Maybe—even if I didn't scratch myself all day and have a serious fascination with housework—I was at least as weird, or worse. I shut the ocean behind us with a click.

The house was still quiet. In the living room, Edmund had abandoned his television snakes and was playing with a dump truck on the floor. Granda was watching the Weather Channel. He spent most of his time napping and studying the weather. He didn't seem to care whether he was listening to news about thunderstorms in Oregon or about heatstroke in Oklahoma. "Hey, Granda," I said. He lifted his hand in a slow-motion salute.

"Oh, Thea, I meant to tell you," Nenna said, "you got a card from your parents yesterday." She started picking up coffee mugs and bundles of knitting and Edmund's art projects. "Here it is. It's addressed to you, but since it's a postcard, a few pair of eyes have already seen it."

I picked up the card. On the front was a picture of the Minneapolis skyline: a cluster of tall blue-gray buildings with the white mushroom of the stadium squatting in front of them. *Dear Thea.* I recognized my father's printing. He always printed. *We hope you are being kind to your Grumman relatives and to yourself. Keep us posted. We'll see you soon.* At the bottom of the card, squeezed under the address, was a single sentence from my mother, in script. *Are you working on the notebook of truths?*

Nenna put her broom away in the kitchen. She washed her hands and started taking the pits out of a pound of cherries. Granda couldn't eat them if they had pits.

I studied the postcard. I had talked to my parents only once ("Hi, Mom, yes, I'm here, and I'm being polite to everyone") since I'd been in Port Harbor. They were sort of old-fashioned that way: they liked the idea of cards and letters. I read my mother's sentence again. What on earth had she been thinking? Now everyone would know I was keeping a notebook. And they would all want to talk about it, and they would probably want to read it, or at least find out what it was.

Truth #28: I have never told anyone what happened at Three Mile Creek.

"Try one of these," Nenna said. She plucked a cherry from the top of the pile and fed it to me. It was dark and sweet.

"Sometimes my parents make a big deal out of things," I said, looking at the postcard. There was no doubt about it: I was going to have to destroy the notebook. Maybe I could burn it, or flush it down the toilet.

Truth #29: I thought my parents would find out somehow. Why didn't they find out?

"They always think there's something going on," I said. "They're always asking me questions."

Nenna smiled. The juice from the cherries ran from her fingers to her wrinkled elbows.

"It's pretty annoying, actually." I picked through the cherries, eating a few of the best-looking specimens. "I kind of wish they would leave me alone."

The baby monitor on the counter let out a squeak. "Whoops. That must be Ralph waking up," Nenna said. "Do you want to go check on him?"

I was feeling crabby. A bad mood was gathering like a cloud inside my head. "I don't know how to check on him."

"There's no *how* about it," Nenna said. The TV predicted rain in Miami. "If he's asleep, just leave him there. If he's awake, you can pick him up."

"But what if he cries?"

She rinsed off the cherries. Her short thin hair was like a silver cap on her head. "I'll give you a little demonstration." She washed her hands and led me down the hall.

"I don't think I'm going to have kids when I get older," I said. "I probably won't get married, either. I'm probably just going to live by myself." We walked up the stairs. "I mean, some people probably like having big families, and they like having friends. I just want to be by myself and be normal." I realized that I wasn't making a lot of sense, but I couldn't stop talking. "The problem with our family is that it's probably impossible to grow up to be normal. I mean, most people don't alphabetize the groceries"—I had seen Phoebe do this—"or play games at dinner. And what about Ralph? What if Ralph doesn't want to be a Creature of Habit? What if he just wants to be a regular person?"

"Shhh." Nenna stopped and turned toward me. She put her hand on my shoulder. "Theodora Elizabeth," she said. Half her face was in shadow. "Did you know that your parents were nervous at first about giving you such a long name?"

"No." I was ashamed of myself, but I wasn't sure why.

"They were. Eight syllables." Nenna opened the door to her room, and together we walked in and saw Ralph struggling on his stomach in the cage of his crib. His arms and legs were paddling away, but they weren't getting him anywhere. He was pale and fleshy in his T-shirt and diaper. I thought he looked like a bug—like a little white grub.

"They worried that they should try to find something shorter," Nenna said. "Or something easier to pronounce." She pushed a couple of buttons and lowered one side of the crib. "But finally they realized that they didn't want to give you a baby's name, or a little girl's name; they wanted to give you the name of the person they hoped you would grow up to be. And so that's what they did. And you're filling that name, one piece at a time—all eight admirable syllables."

She leaned over Ralph's mattress. "Who's my boy? Where's Ralph? Where's my sweetcake?" Nenna's voice was a song. She scooped Ralph up and settled him against her neck. He was still half-asleep; his bald head bobbled back and forth. "Hold out your arms for him."

I did what she told me. Ralph squiggled softly against my chest.

"I want you to promise me something," Nenna said. "When Ralph grows up, I want you to tell him that he should be proud of himself. I want you to tell him that his family loves him. That they will always love him, and they will stand by him no matter what. Can you do that?"

I nodded. Something rose up inside me, some sort of airy little elevator lifting off from my stomach.

"There. See how he trusts you?" Nenna said.

I patted Ralph's fat little wrist with a finger and his eyes flicked open. They were round and blue, as if he were surprised to wake up and find himself in the world.

CHAPTER ELEVEN

☆

It wasn't easy, swallowing paper. I had heard about people doing it, chewing up entire sheets of loose-leaf and forcing the wet gobs of pulp down their throats. But I couldn't do it. I was sitting on the closed lid of the toilet, my mother's notebook of truths in my lap and a thick and gummy soup on my tongue. I felt like I'd eaten a mouthful of paste—the kind from the jar that we used to use in kindergarten.

"Thea?"

I gagged on a wad of paper and coughed. "What?" Why couldn't I be left alone for ten minutes?

"I'm back. Did you get my note?" It was Jocelyn. Who else?

I scraped the mess from my tongue with a toothbrush. I wasn't eating my notebook—not yet. But I was thinking about eating it. I had decided to experiment by trying to eat an envelope first. It was a fairly small envelope, and I figured if I could get it down, I could work my way up to some thicker paper. "Yes, I got your note," I said through the door. I coughed, then spat in the sink.

"Are you throwing up?" I could tell that Jocelyn was standing about an inch away from the door. Her whispery voice was like a needle.

"No. I'll be out in a minute." I looked in the mirror over the sink and saw that my face was red from coughing. Normally I was sort of pale, my skin the color of new cement. My hair was an in-between shade that my mother called auburn. I wiped a splotch of chewed-up paper off my cheek.

"I have to use the bathroom," Jocelyn said.

"Go use a different one." I coughed again, then rinsed my mouth out with water.

"Are you still throwing up? Should I go get Nenna?"

"I am *not* throwing up," I said. "Just use a different bathroom."

"But—Thea?"

"Go. Away. Jocelyn." I heard a gentle scraping against the door.

I dried my hands on the back of my shorts and picked up my notebook. To eat it or not to eat it? The paper was thick, with little specks of something running through it. Maybe they were wood chips? Or leaves? What if they were poisonous? I ran my hand over the cushiony blue cover, then fit my index finger into the center of the star on the front. *You'll feel better if you use this*, my mother had said.

I picked up a pen.

Truth #30: The world record for holding your breath is over eight minutes.

I closed the notebook, using my finger to hold my place. Did I feel any better? On the other side of the bathroom window, seagulls were gliding toward the ocean on an early breeze.

Truth #31: Gwen and I tried to hold our breath by plugging our noses. We timed ourselves by the clock in her kitchen. I only got to forty-three seconds, and I felt like my head was about to explode.

"Thea?" It was Jocelyn again. "The downstairs bathrooms are both full. Somebody's using them. Nenna's taking a shower."

I turned the page and clicked the little plastic button on the top of my pen.

Truth #32:

"I have to go to the bathroom *right now*," Jocelyn whispered. "I can't wait."

"Hold your horses." Reluctantly, I shut the notebook. Thirty-one truths. Sixty-nine more to go. Maybe when I got to one hundred some kind of door would open in my head and I would never again in my entire life have to think about—

"Thea!"

"Okay, I'm coming." I ran some water in the sink, then opened the cabinet underneath it to look for a towel. And there it was, as if I'd been searching for it all along: the perfect hiding place for my notebook. Behind the extra rolls of toilet paper and the boxes of tissues and the bars of soap and the stack of hand towels, there was a broken board. The back wall of the cabinet was cracked and loose. I wrapped the notebook in a garbage bag to keep it clean, then slid a piece of the board aside and hid the notebook between the cabinet and the wall. For added security, I plucked two hairs from my head and set them on top of the broken board. I closed the cabinet again. Like magic: no notebook. Then I unlocked the bathroom door and opened it as if inviting an honored guest into my home.

Jocelyn stood on one foot in the hallway. She peered into the bathroom. "What were you doing in there?"

"Just using the bathroom. I thought you were in a hurry."

"I am. But why were you in there for so long if you aren't sick?"

"I was smoking cigarettes." A purple lie—diversion. "I didn't want anyone to see me."

"Oh." Jocelyn hurried past. "Cigarettes aren't good for you."

I told her I was trying to quit ("It's really hard once you get hooked on them," I said), and she shut the door.

During the next couple of days, we rode our Granda's trike all over Port Harbor. I pedaled Jocelyn to the harbor lighthouse (it wasn't open, but we walked around it), to the broken-down fishing pier (also closed), and to the Fairyland miniature golf course, where a life-sized Snow White and the seven dwarfs danced in a circle around the eighteenth hole. At Jocelyn's insistence, we also spent some time lurking outside the hotel where Celia worked. I didn't see anything very interesting, but Jocelyn claimed to have spotted Ellen's car on the street. It might have been Ellen's; I wasn't sure.

"Aren't you getting tired of secrets and spying?" I asked.

"No." Jocelyn swatted a bug on her shoulder. "Celia was talking to someone on the phone last night," she said.

"Hmm." I turned a corner on the trike; we didn't have enough money for miniature golf, so I was pedaling all the way to the boardwalk again.

"It was the middle of the night. I woke up because I heard her talking." Jocelyn held on to the sides of the basket when we came to a bump. "And it wasn't the first time, either. I bet she's talked to both our parents."

"Why would Celia call our parents in the middle of the night, Jocelyn?" I asked.

"I don't know," she said. "But I heard her."

"She wouldn't have talked to my parents without telling me."

"Yes, she would have." Jocelyn turned halfway around in her seat. "I think I heard her say the name Fred a couple of times. And that's your dad's name."

"I know what my dad's name is," I said. We pushed the trike up the wooden ramp and rode past the haunted house, the spin-paint booth, and the arcades, which, as usual, were full of boys in black T-shirts, all pounding away at a huge assortment of beeping machines.

Jocelyn said her legs were stiff and she wanted to get down. I parked the trike by the metal railing at the edge of the boardwalk and tied it up loosely with the bungee cord. We sat down on a bench. A lot of the benches had metal plaques on them: the plaque on ours read, IN LOVING MEMORY OF HARRY, WHO LOVED THE SEA. I wondered if Granda would ever have a plaque. Then I tried to erase that thought from my mind.

Two old women in flowered dresses went into the fudge shop and came out with an enormous cone of blue cotton candy. They tore off pieces of the fluffy sugar with their fingers, then tipped their heads back and laughed.

"That's where Aunt Ellen and Aunt Celia were when we saw them. Right over there." Jocelyn pointed. Directly across from us were a paperback bookstore, a bakery, the frozen custard booth, the fortune-teller's booth, the man who painted people's names on grains of rice, and an office that said PORT HARBOR REALTY. "I wonder what they were doing."

"Maybe they were buying something to eat," I said. "They probably both like frozen custard."

"They wouldn't come all the way to the boardwalk for frozen custard." Jocelyn fidgeted beside me on the bench. I could tell that she itched. She had taken to wearing a pair of thin white gloves with little pearl buttons at the wrist. Nenna had bought them for her with the idea that Jocelyn would wear them only at night, so that she wouldn't scratch herself in her sleep. But Jocelyn seemed to like wearing them. She wore them all day.

"Maybe they were buying something to read," I said, looking at the bookstore. "Or maybe Aunt Celia's getting married." I remembered my dream about Mr. Hanover and the bridesmaid fish. "They sell wedding cakes at the bakery. Maybe she's secretly engaged to a man named Fred, and that's who she was talking to last night."

"Really?" Jocelyn's eyes were wide. "Do you really think she's getting married?"

"No," I said. "I just made that up."

"Oh. What's a reality office?" Jocelyn asked.

"*Realty*," I said, looking at the sign between the bookstore and the custard shop. "It's a place where you go to buy a house. Or maybe to sell one."

"Are Celia and Ellen selling Nenna and Granda's house?"

"No," I said. "They wouldn't sell it. Anyway, they can't; it isn't theirs to sell. It's Nenna and Granda's."

"Probably no one would buy it anyway," Jocelyn said. "It's kind of old-fashioned."

I agreed that it was. I studied the blue and white sign on the office door: PORT HARBOR REALTY. "Here's what I think," I said. "I think you should stop worrying about other people's secrets. First of all, they might not exist, and second of all, maybe if you didn't worry about them so much, your rash would get better." I leaned back against Harry-who-loved-the-sea. "Besides, when your parents get back, you can just ask your mother if anything unusual is going on, and if there is, she'll tell you."

"She *won't* tell me," Jocelyn said as a silver ice cream cart rumbled by.

"Maybe your dad will tell you," I said.

But Jocelyn just tucked her legs under the bench.

"Are you sure you want to be wearing those gloves?" I asked. "Aren't they uncomfortable?"

No answer.

A little girl walked past us carrying a hermit crab in a cage.

"Maybe Aunt Celia and Aunt Ellen were getting their fortunes told," Jocelyn said. She nodded toward the fortune-teller's booth.

I tried to picture my sturdy aunts sitting down beneath the sequined sign to get their palms read.

Jocelyn rebuttoned her glove at the wrist. "Do you think she really knows what will happen to you?"

"Who, the fortune-teller?" Just a few feet outside Madam Carla's booth, a teenage couple held hands, the boy digging into the pocket of his jeans and coming up with a fistful of money. "I doubt it," I said. "She's probably just a regular person wearing a scarf and big earrings."

"But those people believe in her," Jocelyn said. "I think she knows things." The girl pushed the boy forward, her palm between his shoulder blades. "I think she can probably help people."

"She isn't a nurse, Jocelyn," I said.

The teenage couple sat down.

"I just wish she didn't have to look at your hands to tell your fortune," Jocelyn said. Her own gloved hands were folded in her lap. Her rash was definitely getting worse. It had spread to the insides of her elbows and the backs of her knees.

We sat on the bench for a little while, then split a lemonade and a giant soft pretzel and walked back to the trike.

"It's hot." Jocelyn lifted her bushy hair off the back of her neck. All week the weather had been getting warmer.

"You can go swimming when we get back," I said. "I could stand near the water and watch you."

"No, that's okay." She fiddled with her bungee cord. "Can we ride past the hotel on the way home? I think it's a shortcut."

"Fine with me," I said. "But I wouldn't call it a shortcut."

Truth #32: Three Mile Creek wasn't a shortcut, either. Walking home by the main road and the gas station probably would have been faster.

Jocelyn and I rode to the end of the boardwalk and then retraced our path, riding past the Ferris wheel and the Skee-Ball and the sign for the world's best Philly cheesesteak.

"I think it was definitely your dad that Aunt Celia was talking to," Jocelyn said. "You should try to find out what they were saying. Then you could write it in your secret notebook."

"Celia wasn't talking to my dad. And I'm not going to write it in my notebook."

"Why not?"

I stopped pedaling as we glided toward the bakery and the realty office and the custard stand and the fortune-teller. "Because the notebook is supposed to make me feel better," I said.

"Why do you feel bad?" Jocelyn asked.

I didn't answer. We were close to the fortune-teller's booth. Madam Carla was alone in her little kiosk.

"Don't you wish you could know what's going to happen to people ahead of time?" Jocelyn asked.

Madam Carla looked up and seemed to lock eyes with us. KNOW YOUR FUTURE. With a long and skinny index finger, she pointed above her head at the glittering sign just as we rode by.

CHAPTER TWELVE

☆

I didn't really think that Celia was making midnight phone calls to my parents. What would she talk to them about? Would she call to tell them that I did a lousy job on the laundry? Would she ask about the book of truths? I tried not to imagine their conversation, but I couldn't help it.

Celia: *Oh, so Thea's a liar. That makes sense. Of course we were wondering.*

My mother: *We've been trying to train her to stop, but you know it isn't easy at this age. I bought her a notebook, but she—*

Celia: *That's what she's been hiding, then. Ellen and I thought she was fairly unusual, even for a Grumman.*

My mother: *Do you think she'll grow out of it?*

"I'm going to give my parents a call," I announced on Saturday morning. "I'll just check in and see what they're up to."

Nenna and Celia were straightening up the living room, Granda was reading (he held a book in his hands but had his eyes closed), and Ellen was hovering around the recycling bin. She had taken a dozen plastic containers from the bottom of the bin, and she was flattening them one by one on the kitchen floor.

I picked up the phone. It was an old-fashioned phone with a very short cord, so you had to stand next to it when you were talking. "I figure since no one else has talked to them, I should call and say hi," I said. "Just to check in. Is that all right?"

"Of course it's all right. Go ahead, Thea," Nenna said. Celia had her back to me. I dialed.

Usually on Saturday mornings my parents did errands—they went to the dry cleaner or the farmers' market or the grocery store—so I wasn't sure anyone would be home. But my father answered on the second ring. "Grummans," he said, and I immediately pictured him in our kitchen: he was probably in the breakfast nook with the morning paper spread out in front of him, his square black glasses perched on his head.

Truth #33: Sometimes I wonder whether my parents wish they had a better daughter. They probably wanted someone tiny and cute, a girl who would come home and do her homework without being asked and then go off with twenty of her best friends to cheerleading practice.

"Hey, Dad," I said. I had to turn toward the wall because of a sudden lump in my throat. "It's me. Thea."

"Well, hey there yourself," my father said. I could barely hear him because Ellen was crushing another container, which made a *whooomph* sound when it collapsed beneath her heel.

"Is everything okay?" my father asked. "Are you having fun?"

"Sure," I said. The wallpaper in the kitchen was printed with blue and green teacups. "I just wanted to see what you were up to."

"Your mother's grocery shopping. And I'm getting ready to fix the screen door. It's pretty exciting here, overall. Is everybody taking good care of you?"

"Yeah."

Whoooomph. Ellen crushed an applesauce container.

My father told me a long and involved story about what had happened to the screen door, and how he had already tried to fix it twice, and what the person at the hardware store had told him about the new kind of bracket he should use.

"Are you still there?" he asked.

"I'm here."

"And everything's fine in Port Harbor?"

I told him it was.

"Over and out, then." He asked me to say hello to everyone, and he hung up the phone.

I felt like an idiot. I should have just asked him if

he'd talked to Celia. But what if he had? Wasn't he allowed to talk to his sister?

"Is there any news in Minnesota?" Ellen asked. She had flattened all the plastic within reach and seemed to be looking around the kitchen for something to crush.

"No, not really," I said. "My mother was out grocery shopping."

"I think I'm going out myself," Ellen said. "Celia, didn't I give you the—" She stopped and made a twisting motion with her hand.

Jocelyn had wandered into the kitchen behind me.

"Oh. That's right," Celia said. "I'll get it." She started rummaging through her purse. She found something inside it and tossed it to Ellen, but her aim was off. There was a clink, like a single high note on a piano, as something landed by my foot on the floor.

It was a key—a single key on a silver key chain. I picked it up. Jocelyn was at my side in a split second. We looked at the little white tag attached to the key chain. In neat black letters it said 21 BAY.

Ellen held out her hand. "I'll take that, Thea. Thank you."

I gave her the key.

"Where are you going, Aunt Ellen?" Jocelyn asked. "Can I please go with you?"

Ellen tucked the key into her pocket. "Another time."

100

☆

Truth #34:

"Why didn't she let me go with her?" Jocelyn whined.

"I don't know." I was back in the bathroom, trying to work on my notebook. I could see Jocelyn's toes through the narrow crack beneath the door.

"But what do you *think*? Thea, tell me."

I waggled my pen above the page. I wondered how many lies the average person told in a week. Or even a year. I imagined what it would be like if everyone had their own container of lies and once they filled it they wouldn't be able to lie anymore. My container was probably overflowing.

"Do you think it was the same key we saw Ellen put in her purse at the boardwalk?" Jocelyn asked.

It had to be, I thought. And what the heck was 21 Bay?

She rattled the doorknob. "Are you coming out soon?"

"Leave me alone. I need to pee and I can't do it if you're standing there waiting."

There was a pause of about six seconds. "Aunt Phoebe says if you're smoking cigarettes in there you should definitely stop."

"Phoebe said what?"

"She said cigarettes are bad for you and they'll give

you cancer and if you burn down Nenna and Granda's house it's going to be very hard for her to forgive you." Jocelyn tapped her finger against the door. "Thea?"

"*What?*"

"Maybe something bad is happening," she said.

"Nothing bad is happening."

"How do you know?"

I wrapped up the notebook and tucked it back in its hiding place. I flushed the toilet (even though I hadn't used it) and opened the door. "So you told Phoebe that I was smoking cigarettes?"

Jocelyn shrugged. Her shoulder bones were the size of Ping-Pong balls.

I thought about lecturing her for being a tattletale, but since I hadn't really been smoking, it didn't seem worth the trouble. Besides, I reminded myself that Nenna thought I was being nice to her.

"Why do you always take so long in the bathroom?" she asked.

"Because the bathroom is great," I said. "I love the bathroom. It's so cozy. It's probably my favorite room in the house."

"Really? I like Liam and Austin's room better," Jocelyn said.

We went downstairs. In the living room, Granda was watching TV (the forecaster was calling for desertlike weather in Phoenix) and Nenna was playing crazy eights with Edmund. "Do you girls want to play with us?" she asked. Jocelyn did. It was hard to resist Nenna when she was playing a game. She could be playing the stupidest game in the world, but she would laugh and exclaim the entire time, as if in all her life she had never dreamed of having so much fun.

I made a big stack of peanut-butter-and-honey-on-cracker sandwiches and went out to the deck with a paperback. I sat in a deck chair, my calves flattened out like two pancakes in front of me, and watched as a couple of girls about my age raced each other across the sand and into the ocean.

Truth #34: I really miss Gwen.

I read a few pages, realized I hadn't paid any attention to what they said, and then read them again. What were Celia and Ellen doing with that key?

"Hey, ugly. What's up?"

I shaded my eyes and turned around.

Liam climbed the three wooden steps to the deck and stood beside me, a yellow surfboard creating a puddle of shade at his feet. "Are you planning to sit here all day by yourself?"

"I might. Why?"

"No reason." He reached for one of my peanut-butter-and-honey-on-cracker sandwiches. "I just thought you might want to learn how to surf."

Liam and Austin were good surfers. During the summer they surfed almost every day, whether the waves were six feet high or six inches. Ellen said they had salt water in their veins instead of blood. When I was younger, I used to stand at the edge of the water and watch them, a gray coil of ocean rising behind them to graze their shoulders.

"I'm not wearing my bathing suit," I said.

"You could get up on your hind legs and go into the house and *put* it on." A dribble of honey fell from his lips and landed on my deck chair.

"Liam, do you think anything strange is going on around here?" I asked.

"I don't know. Do you mean strange like the regular kind of strange, or something different?"

I accidentally put my arm in the honey. "I mean something that's happening but nobody's talking about it," I said.

"Like what?"

"I'm not sure. It probably doesn't matter. Never mind." Why did I care about Jocelyn's ridiculous schemes, anyway?

Austin was thumping his way down the steps. "Are you ready, loser?" He grabbed his own surfboard.

"In a couple of minutes," Liam said. "Thea's coming with us."

Austin stopped in his tracks, looking as if someone had slapped him.

The ocean was a hundred yards away, shining like a giant bowl of cut glass. "That's okay," I said. "You guys go ahead. I'll watch from here."

"Are you sure?" Liam licked his fingers.

I told him I was. "I don't have a bathing suit. I forgot to pack one."

Austin cocked his head. "You came to the beach— for three weeks—without a bathing suit? What did you bring with you? A down jacket?" He cackled at his own little joke, then reached out a long tan arm and swooped up the rest of my cracker sandwiches. "Man, we don't have any decent food around here. I couldn't find any donuts."

"And there's no bologna," Liam said. "Tragic."

I heard a *click-clack*ing noise behind us: Jocelyn was coming down the outdoor stairs, carrying her purse and wearing her patent leather shoes. She held the handrail (she was still wearing gloves) with every step.

"Ah! The family royalty," Austin said. "It's always a privilege." He put down his surfboard and fell to his knees. His hair was hanging over his face like a dirty blond curtain. "Your Majesty!"

"Be quiet," Jocelyn told him. "Nenna's watching you from the window. And she said she wants you both to be careful while you surf."

"Hey, Nenna!" Austin yelled. "We're going to catch some big ones!" He stood up and waved. Then he turned to Liam. "Are you ready to go yet? Or are you going to stand here flapping your lips all day?"

Liam bonked me lightly on the head with his surfboard. "Are you sure you don't want to come? You could swim in your clothes."

"She can't," Jocelyn said. "Thea can't go into the ocean at all. She's allergic to jellyfish."

"She's what?"

"They don't even have to sting her," Jocelyn added. "If she just goes in the water and they're around, her whole body swells up. She gets enormous."

There was a silence while Liam and Austin apparently mulled this idea over.

"I might actually pay good money to see that," Austin finally said. "Does she look like the whale in *Pinocchio*?"

Liam was muttering to himself. "Allergic to *jellyfish*?"

"Just forget it," I told him. "I don't want to surf."

Austin picked up a crab's claw and sniffed it, then threw it at his brother.

"Hey, Liam," I said. "You and Austin don't know anything about twenty-one Bay, do you?"

"I don't think so." Liam tightened the string on his bathing suit, a pair of orange trunks that hung below his knees. "What is it, some kind of dorky girl band?"

"No. I don't know what it is. I just heard the name. I thought you might have heard of it."

He shrugged. "Nope."

Daintily, Jocelyn climbed onto the deck chair next to mine. "I don't think they know anything," she said, as if Liam and Austin were nowhere around.

"Come on, let's get out of here." Austin elbowed Liam, then nodded to Jocelyn. "Au revoir, Your Majesty."

"Don't call me *Your Majesty*," Jocelyn said.

Austin bowed, carving a flowery gesture into the air with his hand.

Jocelyn and I sat back in our deck chairs. To our left, half a dozen gray and white seagulls were tussling over some kind of carcass. "You shouldn't have asked them that," Jocelyn said.

"Why not? I thought you wanted to find out what the secret was."

She straightened her glove. "I thought you didn't believe there was a secret at all."

CHAPTER THIRTEEN

☆

If there was a secret—and maybe there was—it wasn't any of our business. That was what I told Jocelyn. And *if* there was a secret, it was probably something boring. That was the way secrets were with adults. Maybe Ellen was sending for information about colleges for C-minus students like Austin, and she had a key to a private mailbox. Or maybe Celia was going to start her own business—a bed-and-breakfast or a pancake house.

"I don't think a pancake house would be boring," Jocelyn said.

I told her that was just an example. Maybe Celia and Ellen were going to start up a laundry service. "Grumman's Laundo-rama," I said. "We Put Wind in Your Sheets."

"And in your pillowcases," Jocelyn said. We seemed to be getting used to each other. From all the time we spent on the tricycle, I was used to the sight of her fluffy hair and her bungee cord, and her gloved hands gripping the wicker basket. She was probably used to my breathing on the back of her neck, and the squeak of the seat when I sat back down. Together we learned the location of every soft pretzel stand and water ice store in the town of Port Harbor. And while we rode, we talked about what the island probably looked like from above: a narrow cigar-shaped piece of sand tied to the rest of the state of New Jersey by two fragile bridges.

We developed a kind of unspoken agreement. Jocelyn left me alone (most of the time) about my notebook, and I didn't interfere with her snooping and spying; I pedaled almost every afternoon right past the hotel where Aunt Celia worked. And if we stopped in the shade for a few minutes so that Jocelyn could look for Ellen's car, what did it matter? We weren't bothering anyone. We were just riding, and killing time. I doubted anyone knew.

☆

"Thea? I was wondering if I could talk to you for a few minutes," Ellen said.

It was nine o'clock, and Nenna had just sent Jocelyn and Edmund to bed. I had gone out to the back porch with a book of science fiction stories, and I was reading about a group of people in a spaceship who discovered that the planet they were traveling to had exploded.

"What do you want to talk about?" I asked.

"Doubles." Ellen was standing in front of me, hands on her hips. "I'm just wondering whether you believe in doubles."

"In what?" I dog-eared a page of the book and put it down.

"Some people say that everyone in the world has at least one person who looks a lot like them," Ellen said. "Celia thought she might have seen your double this afternoon, in the parking lot outside the hotel."

"Oh." The sun was setting. Over Ellen's shoulder, the ocean was calm and pink, almost transparent. "It wasn't my double."

Ellen leaned against the railing. "That's what I thought. It seemed like too much of a coincidence for your double and Jocelyn's double to be traveling through downtown Port Harbor together."

"I guess that would have been a coincidence. But it wasn't," I said, "since those weren't our doubles." An assortment of moths were hammering against the yellow light above my head.

Celia opened the sliding door and came toward us, a cup of coffee and a newspaper in her hand. "What a beautiful night," she said. "Do you mind if I join you?"

I looked at the headline splashed across her paper: *Two-Headed Dog Bites Man.* And I thought *I* was reading science fiction.

"Put your coffee down, Celia," Ellen said. "We're going for a walk."

The three of us went down the steps and over the bulkhead and around the clumps of dune grass that sprouted up along the beach like little green swords. At night the sand on the beach was different: it felt powdery and cool, as if someone had poured it through a giant sifter. Ellen took Celia's elbow and they walked ahead of me toward the water. I watched their two bulky shapes slowly wander away.

Finally Celia stopped in front of me and turned around. "You and Jocelyn have been doing some traveling."

"I wouldn't call it traveling," I said.

Truth #35: You can't see Three Mile Creek until you're almost on top of it. It's cut deep into the earth, about ten feet below a long curving path of rocks and trees.

"We all know that seven-year-olds aren't easy to spend a lot of time with," Ellen said. "And Jocelyn can certainly be—"

"Determined," Celia interrupted.

"I was going to say *difficult*. In any case—"

"We do appreciate that you're spending time with her," Celia finished. "It's very good of you, Thea."

I wanted to tell her that they hadn't given me much of a choice, but I didn't have time to interrupt.

"Let's get to the point," Ellen said. "Shall we?"

We walked past the lifeguard stand in the direction

of the jetty, a long black column of rocks that stuck out into the water. "We want to make sure you aren't encouraging her," Celia said. "That's the main thing."

"Encouraging her in what?"

"We're not talking about rudeness or real misbehavior," Celia went on. "She's so well behaved most of the time. That's why it's such a shame when—"

"She followed me to the drugstore yesterday," Ellen said.

"Jocelyn did? Well, she follows everyone. She likes to spy on people," I said. "That isn't my fault." I stepped on a shell and stopped to pluck it from between my toes.

"She isn't getting to the hotel by herself, is she?" Ellen asked.

They had both turned toward me, but it had gotten dark and I could barely see their faces. Behind them, the ocean looked heavier and thicker, more mysterious.

Truth #36: Gwen wasn't allowed to go to the creek by herself until she was ten. We thought her mother was overprotective.

Celia coughed. "The problem here is that there are issues that—"

Ellen interrupted her. "What it boils down to, Thea, is that Jocelyn's parents aren't here, so it's up to others to look after her welfare."

"Thea's parents aren't here, either," Celia pointed out.

"Jocelyn's much younger than Thea," Ellen said. "She isn't prepared for—"

Celia cut her off. "We just have to be careful."

"Okay," I said.

We walked in silence for a little while.

"Careful about what, though?" I asked. "Because I don't think I understand what you're saying."

We had reached the jetty. The rocks were black and shiny and enormous, a row of them extending into the ocean like a giant arm.

"Should we start to head back?" Ellen put a heavy hand on my shoulder. We turned around, the breeze blowing toward us.

"Here's what we're saying," Celia said. "It would be better for both of you not to go creeping around town, poking into things that, well . . ."

"Things that what?"

"We can't go into detail," Ellen said. "It's obviously an awkward situation."

"You think it's awkward that Jocelyn's spying on you," I said.

"That's right. We do," Celia said. "Because we're trying to consider what's best for Jocelyn. And for you, too, Thea. Even though there's not much we can say on the subject."

"What subject?" I asked.

"In fact, all we can tell you," Celia said, "is that—"

"All we can tell you," Ellen interrupted, "is that it doesn't have anything to do with you personally, Thea. It isn't any of your business."

"Thanks a lot," I said.

Ellen's hand squeezed my neck. "How much longer are you and Jocelyn going to be here? Another five or six days? That's not very long. You can help her find something constructive to do."

"Can you teach her to knit?" Celia asked.

"I don't know how to knit. And I think if you want me to keep an eye on her, you should—" I opened my mouth and then closed it again. How could I ask them if they were keeping a secret when they could ask the same thing of me?

"How much money has Thea earned so far, Celia?" Ellen asked.

"Oh. Probably sixty at least," Celia said. "If we're counting on three hours a day, five days a week—"

"It's more like four hours a day," I said. "Four hours at least."

"At three dollars an hour, that's sixty a week. So I suppose you're already up to a hundred and twenty. A hundred and twenty dollars." Celia whistled.

"Are you really going to pay me?" I asked.

"Why wouldn't we pay you? We just want to make sure that there's no more spying," Ellen said. "Are we agreed?"

I nodded.

"Good," Ellen said. "And of course you don't need to tell Jocelyn about this conversation."

"It's a lovely night for a walk," Celia said.

We started back toward Nenna and Granda's, toward the squares of light that seemed to float above the sand.

CHAPTER FOURTEEN

☆

"I think you had another nightmare last night," Jocelyn said.

I poured myself a bowl of cereal and sliced some bananas on top of it. Did Celia and Ellen count as some kind of nightmare? Maybe they did; I was feeling groggy and disoriented. "Why do you say that?"

"Because you woke me up." Jocelyn plucked a slice of banana, like a fleshy medallion, from the top of my cereal.

Truth #37: Usually in my dreams it's February. I don't have to look at a calendar or even see that it's winter. I can just tell what month it is. In the dream, I just know.

I discovered that we didn't have any milk. What was I supposed to do with a bowl of dry cereal? "Did I talk in my sleep?" I asked Jocelyn. "Was I walking around with my arms out in front of me like Frankenstein's monster?"

"No. You weren't walking."

I ate a spoonful of dry flakes. They made an enormous noise in my skull, like an army marching through a field.

Truth #38: In the dreams, I always have a terrible, heavy feeling. It feels like a thousand hooks are attached to my lungs and someone's tugging on them, trying to pull them out.

I ate another spoonful of dry flakes and looked out the sliding door to the porch. The ocean was calm, as if someone had passed a giant hand across its surface.

Jocelyn was scratching herself again. She had a new patch of eczema at the base of her throat. "Edmund's playing with Brian today," she said.

"Hm." I crunched my cereal.

"So we can go out and explore whenever we want. Nenna says she doesn't need us. And it's going to be nice all day."

"Really?" *It would be better for both of you not to go creeping around town*, Celia had said. And she owed me a hundred and twenty dollars. "It looks like it might rain, though."

Jocelyn shaded her eyes and looked at the cloudless blue sky and the brilliant sun. "It isn't going to rain."

I glanced over at Nenna, who was playing with Ralph. Phoebe had left him behind in his plastic carrier and gone to the dentist. "It *might* rain," I said. "Anyway, I was thinking that we should stay home today for a change. Instead of riding the trike." I felt Jocelyn staring at me. "There are a lot of things we can do around here. Maybe we could work on some arts and crafts."

"Oh, Ralph, you're the handsomest thing," Nenna said. "Oh, bub bub bub."

"Or maybe we could set up a sprinkler," I said. "Or play with water balloons or something." I sounded like an idiot. Who played with water balloons a hundred yards from the ocean? "Besides," I said, dumping the rest of my cereal into the garbage, "my ankle's bothering me. I think I sprained it."

"Did you hurt yourself, Thea?" Even though Nenna was hard of hearing, she seemed to have a grandmotherly radar that went on alert whenever someone was wounded. She turned around, holding Ralph on her hip. Together they looked like a strange two-headed creature. *She used to hold me like that*, I thought.

"I must have stepped in a hole last night." The lie seemed to burn its way up my throat. "People should fill those holes in when they're finished digging them."

"Sit down over here and let me see it." Nenna patted a cushion on the couch, and when I sat, she plopped Ralph down beside me. He immediately turned his pale head and started gumming my arm.

"Is this where it's bothering you?" Nenna squeezed my foot.

I tried to wince. "Kind of."

She moved my toes gently, one at a time. "I don't think it's swollen. We'll just keep an eye on it. Can I get you anything? Maybe some ice? Or a cold drink?"

"No thanks, Nenna."

She patted my leg, then picked Ralph up (he had left a string of drool on my elbow) and carried him into the kitchen, singing "Three Blind Mice."

☆

Truth #39: Gwen and I thought no one else was at the creek that afternoon. But we were wrong.

"You didn't tell me you went out on the beach last night," Jocelyn said.

"What do you mean?" I was feeling rattled.

"You said you stepped in a hole in the sand."

I stood up and stretched, then opened the sliding glass door to the porch. Out on the beach, people were sunning themselves and playing Frisbee and swimming and eating watermelon in the shade of a hundred umbrellas. Sunlight was flashing across the ocean in liquid sparks.

"It doesn't look like your ankle hurts," Jocelyn said. "You aren't limping."

I thought about trying a limp or two, but I couldn't remember which foot I had shown to Nenna. I went

119

down the outdoor stairs and around the side of the house to the front sidewalk. Jocelyn followed me. Someone had left a folding chair by the mailbox. I tried to unfold it, but the hinge was stuck.

"Austin says it isn't true about the jellyfish," Jocelyn said. "He doesn't think you're really allergic." She watched me struggle with the chair. "You have to push that silver button. He says it isn't true about the i-zone, either."

"Ozone." I pushed the button she was pointing to and the chair sprang open. "It might not be completely true," I said. "I might have been exaggerating a little."

A woman with a Chihuahua on a leash was coming toward us. The Chihuahua's eyes stuck out of its head like giant marbles.

"I knew that," Jocelyn said. She watched the little dog trot past, his toenails clicking. "You wouldn't exaggerate if it was something important, though. Like if you were talking about the secret."

I stuck my legs out onto the sidewalk.

"Because you promised," Jocelyn said. "That's how I know. Because you promised to tell me what it was when you figured it out."

"I haven't figured it out," I said. "I don't know anything about a secret. They didn't tell me anything."

Jocelyn found a second folding chair beneath the stairs, dragged it out to the sidewalk, and put it next to mine. She opened it in about two seconds. "Do you mean Aunt Celia and Aunt Ellen? Were they on the beach with you?"

It was probably only nine in the morning, but I was exhausted. "Do you wear other people out like this?" I asked.

She didn't answer. I could tell she was willing to hound me all day.

"All right, fine. I went for a walk with them," I said. "They made me."

"What did they want?"

"Well, first of all, they definitely want you to stop spying. Did you follow Ellen to the drugstore?"

Jocelyn set a pebble on the arm of her chair.

"And they don't want us hanging around the hotel anymore," I said. "But the whole thing was weird."

"What was weird?"

"The whole conversation. They don't want us being curious about anything. We're supposed to stay here during the day."

Jocelyn picked up another pebble. "We don't have to listen to them," she said. "They aren't our parents."

I remembered Ellen saying that they were looking out for Jocelyn's welfare.

"We'll just be more careful," Jocelyn said.

Wasn't that what Celia had told me, out on the beach? "Careful of what?" I asked.

"That they don't see us."

121

I leaned forward in my chair. "Jocelyn, we're riding around town on a giant tricycle. It's hard *not* to see us."

Jocelyn suggested that we could park the trike and walk.

I told her she was being ridiculous.

"No, I'm not."

"Yes, you are. They'll see us. They could probably spot you a mile away because of your hair."

"My hair?" Jocelyn's shadow, on the ground beside me, touched its frizzy head. "I could tie it back. Or you could braid it for me."

Two boys with a kite shaped like a dragon walked past us, arguing on their way to the beach.

"Your hair's too hard to braid," I said. That wasn't a lie. "We're staying here."

☆

I couldn't believe how slow the day was. Jocelyn and I colored in coloring books and made primitive animals out of pipe cleaners and played about a hundred games of solitaire. We ate lunch with Nenna and Granda and froze orange juice in ice cube trays and read Edmund some books. We baked cookies, and almost all of them burned. They looked like flat little pieces of charcoal. ("Did you mean to use the broiler for these, Thea?" Nenna asked.) Not even Liam and Austin would go near them when they were done.

By six o'clock, I was half-asleep on the couch. Celia was setting the table for dinner. "It's time to eat," she said. "Thea? Dad?"

I rubbed my eyes and watched my Granda shuffle inch by inch across the floor, his dark, hard hands lightly knocking against the furniture. It was like he was frozen in there, I thought. Underneath, he was still the same person, but on the surface he was slowly turning into wood.

We found our places.

Phoebe picked up her slip of paper, pulled out her chair, and glanced around the table. "Okay, let's see. Is it degree of tan?" She pointed at Austin and Liam sitting together, a possible end to a spectrum.

"Nope." Celia grinned.

"Jocelyn isn't here yet," Edmund said.

"Shoe size?" Austin reached for a baked potato. He took two, split both of them quickly down the middle, and added butter, salt and pepper, and sour cream. As usual, seeing Liam and Austin eat was like watching a pair of vacuum cleaners suck up a pile of food.

"Annual income?" Uncle Corey asked. He was rocking Ralph's little plastic chair with his foot.

"I'll go get Jocelyn," I said. I went to the bottom of the stairs and shouted, "Jocelyn, are you coming?" No answer. I could see that the bathroom door was closed. I went up and knocked on it. "Jocelyn?"

"Don't come in," a voice said. "I'm not ready."

"Ready for what? We aren't having a beauty pageant

down here; we're eating dinner." I rattled the knob, but the door was locked.

"I'm almost done," she said. "Go away."

"Well, whatever you're doing in there, hurry up. Your food's getting cold." I went back to the table.

"Talkativeness?" Ellen guessed when I sat back down. Obviously Granda and Ralph would have been last in that category.

"There were no good waves today," Liam grumbled. "The water's too calm." He reached for the platter of tomatoes and slid almost all of them onto his plate. "Is there any dessert after this?"

"There are two kinds of pie," Nenna told him.

"Eye color?" Phoebe asked. Everyone stopped eating long enough to glance around the table at each other's eyes.

"Is Jocelyn coming?" Corey asked.

"She said she is." I buttered my roll. "She's in the— oh." Jocelyn stood in the doorway. "Bathroom," I said.

Everyone turned around.

Jocelyn had cut her hair. At least a foot of it, maybe more. She looked like a prisoner or an orphan. I wondered what she had done with the hair. Maybe she had stuffed a large pillow.

Austin opened his mouth, but Celia slammed her elbow into his chest. "Not a word out of you," she said.

"Did you cut your hair, Jocelyn?" Edmund asked. He had a milk mustache.

Jocelyn pulled out her chair and sat down. "I don't think it's even yet," she said. "I might need someone to help me with the back."

When she turned her head, we could see that the hair had been hacked off in enormous clumps. What was left looked like wads of yellow cotton glued to the sides of her head.

A sinking feeling came over me, as if my bones had been filled with cold water.

"Didn't you like the way it looked?" Phoebe asked. "You should have told us."

Jocelyn shrugged.

Ellen was holding an ear of corn in her fist like a weapon.

"Mom? Are you going to eat that?" Liam asked.

Nenna reached across the table, unfolded Jocelyn's napkin, and handed it to her. "I think short hair is very practical," she said. "Especially at the beach. I've kept my hair short for forty years."

"Mom," Celia said. "I think this is different."

"*And* I think Jocelyn's hair will look very nice after someone at a beauty shop touches it up. Maybe tomorrow," Nenna went on. "Maybe Thea wouldn't mind taking her."

I nodded.

"Wonderful," Nenna said. "It's all settled, then. We don't have to discuss it."

"May I be excused now?" I asked.

Austin reached over and took the roll from my plate. "She ate almost everything," he said.

I went out on the beach. I found out later that Celia had seated us according to number of freckles: Liam had the most and Ralph, his face as smooth and white as a bowl of cream, had none at all.

CHAPTER FIFTEEN

☆

"Okay, so I guess I'm curious," Liam said. He had followed me out to the beach after dinner. "Did you dare her to shave her head or something?"

"No. I just told her—oh, forget it." I sat down on the ruins of a sand castle. "You and Austin go to work every day. I have to babysit. You don't know what it's like."

"I helped babysit you once," Liam said. He did a handstand. "You were in a playpen or something, and I gave you a bottle."

"You gave me a bottle?"

"Yup." He lost his balance and tipped over. "And I remember I was jealous, because Austin got to push you around the block in a stroller. I was mad because he was allowed to and I wasn't."

"*Austin* babysat me?"

Liam brushed some sand off his forehead. "I think

you were right," he said, "the other day on the deck. I think something's happening."

"What's happening?"

"I don't know. I just . . . My mom told me you were acting weird because you were homesick. But you've come here every summer."

"Ellen said I was homesick?"

"And Austin and I thought we'd be going home sometimes on the weekends, but my mom doesn't want to. And now you've got Jocelyn shaving her head."

"She didn't *shave* it," I pointed out.

"Do you know how you can tell when a tidal wave's coming?" Liam sat down next to me, facing the water. "Tidal waves give you a warning. The water pulls back— it pulls away from your feet and from the shore. And all the stuff that was hidden on the bottom is right there in front of you. All the weird rocks and pieces of driftwood and even fish." He picked up a fistful of sand, then opened his fingers and let it go. "I get that feeling sometimes. Like something's coming."

We looked out at the water.

"Do you have that feeling now?" I asked.

"Kind of." He shrugged. "Uh-oh. Heads up."

I turned around. Edmund was running toward us, hopping a little with every other step. He was wearing a long-sleeved button-up shirt that was much too big for him, because Jocelyn had told him he didn't want to get X-rayed by the sun. Now the sun was going down and the sky was pink, but Edmund was still dressed as if it were noon in the Sahara desert. "I came outside to play with you," he announced, as if he were doing us a favor.

Liam reared up and tackled him, grabbing his legs and rolling him over in the sand. "You'd better say *uncle*, or you're a goner."

"Uncle!" said Edmund.

"Wrong!" Liam sat on him. "I'm not your uncle; I'm your cousin. Ha ha!"

Edmund grinned. "I want to find sand crabs," he said. "But someone has to watch me."

Liam helped him up, and both of us followed him to the darker sand at the water's edge. It was the closest I had been to the ocean all year.

Edmund plunged his fingers into the sand, but they came up empty. "I can't find any crabs. Thea, help me." He bounced up and down.

I dug around in the wet sand until I found a tiny dust-colored creature about half an inch long. I handed it to Edmund, but he jumped and dropped it. "It's not going to hurt you," I said. I found the crab again and made Edmund hold it with his palm open. He watched it scuttle across his wrist as if crossing a bridge.

Liam found a slipper shell and a mermaid's purse. "I was trying to remember the number you asked me about out on the deck," he said.

"Do you mean twenty-one Bay?"

"Yeah." He dug a trench with his foot. "It's—I think I might have seen something."

"I need another crab," Edmund said.

"Hang on a second." I grabbed Liam's elbow. "What do you mean, you think you saw something?"

"I'm not sure if I remember it right," Liam said.

I thought of telling him about seeing Celia and Ellen at the boardwalk, and about the key. But Edmund was jumping up and down between us, clamoring for attention. I tried to find him another crab but couldn't; maybe they had all moved on to a better part of the beach in some kind of great sand crab migration.

"Liam, where are you going?" Edmund asked. "I want to play a game with you."

I turned around. Liam was headed back to the house.

"I'll be back," he said, waving to Edmund. "You can play a game with Thea. She likes really long games best. Things that take about a hundred hours. Ask her to teach you how to play Monopoly."

"I don't play Monopoly," I said.

"You used to play, before someone lost all the pieces."

"No, I didn't. I never played." A blue lie—I clenched my teeth.

"Whatever." Liam turned and walked away, his T-shirt flapping in the breeze behind him.

☆

Edmund and I found two or three more crabs, but they were small and sickly. I took him back to the house and Nenna told him he needed to get ready for bed. And she asked me to go upstairs to check on Jocelyn.

130

"I'm sure she's okay, Nenna," I said. But because it was Nenna who had done the asking, I went to check on Jocelyn anyway.

At the top of the steps, I heard water running. "Jocelyn?" She was in the bathroom. I knocked. "What are you doing in there?"

The water went off, then on. "I'm brushing my teeth."

"Can I come in?"

"No. You never let me come in."

"That's different," I said.

"No, it isn't." She opened the door. She wore a white nightgown with a ruffle at her knobby knees, and she held a toothbrush in her hand, but it didn't look wet. It was a shock all over again to see her hair. It was flat in some places and pointy in others. She looked like Bozo the Clown's younger sister.

"Go ahead, tell me," I said. "Why did you do it?" I watched her squeeze a perfect stripe of toothpaste onto her brush.

"Because." She put the toothbrush into her mouth, then took it out again. "You said they'd recognize me."

I looked at the black and white tile floor beneath our feet. Some of the black tiles were missing, which always drove me crazy; the zigzag pattern was all thrown off. "You're talking about Celia and Ellen," I said.

Jocelyn brushed, then spat daintily into the sink. She nodded.

"But both of them saw you." I was speaking patiently

and slowly. "They just saw you at dinner. So both of them know that you cut your hair. How in the world are they not going to recognize you?" I wanted to strangle her. But first I wanted to strangle myself.

Jocelyn set her toothbrush down on the counter. "A woman's hair is what makes her beautiful," she said.

"Who told you that?"

"I don't remember."

I studied our reflections in the bathroom mirror. Jocelyn looked forlorn and lonesome, like a sheep that had been badly clipped and sent away from the herd. "It might not look bad after someone fixes it," I said. I patted a tuft of her hair and a few wiry strands came away in my fingers. "Does it feel strange?"

"Kind of." She took the hair from my hand and threw it into the basket beneath the sink. We turned off the light and made our way to the attic. Jocelyn wiped off the bottoms of her feet and got into bed. I tucked her in, making her covers as tight as the skin on a drum.

"I wonder what souvenirs your parents are buying you," I said, trying to cheer her up.

She didn't answer.

"Maybe it's something to wear. Maybe clothes from Italy."

"They're probably just regular clothes," Jocelyn said.

"I bet they're not. They wouldn't have told you they were bringing you something if it wasn't going to be good. Maybe they'll bring you a new purse and new shoes."

"I don't want anything new," Jocelyn said. "I like the things I already have."

☆

"Thea?"

Truth #40: When I got back from Three Mile Creek that afternoon, I went in the back door and ran up the steps and made sure my parents didn't see me.

"Thea!"

Someone was clutching my shoulder. I was still trying to run up the steps. There were so many steps.

"You have to wake up. Someone's out on the porch," Jocelyn hissed.

Truth #41: I was so cold, it was hard to move. But I quickly got changed and put my clothes into a plastic bag in the back of my closet.

"Thea!" Jocelyn was kneeling on my bed, pinning me to the sheets.

The attic was dark.

I sat up with a jolt, sweaty and out of breath. "It's probably just birds, Jocelyn," I said.

"It isn't birds. I can hear people talking. They were throwing something at our window."

I tried to push my hair out of my face, but my arm was asleep. It felt like a dead thing fastened to my body.

"Don't worry about it," I said, pulling my dead hand out from under me. "It's probably just—"

Something hit the window screen and bounced off. I could hear someone laughing on the porch below.

"Move," I said. I pushed Jocelyn out of the way and threw off the covers. We tiptoed across the attic to the window.

"Do you think it's Nenna?" Jocelyn whispered.

Something hit the screen just in front of us. I heard a rocking chair being dragged across the floor. I tried to look straight down at the porch, but all I saw was a dark rectangular shadow.

"You'd better get out of here," I said to the shadow, trying to make my voice low. "We've already called the police."

"No, you haven't. You don't have a phone up there." It was Liam. "Just open the screen."

Carefully I loosened the latch on the screen and pushed it open. Jocelyn and I poked our heads through the gap and saw Liam and Austin on the porch below. "It's the middle of the night," I said. "What are you doing?"

"It isn't the middle of the night; it's eleven-forty-five," Austin said. "I just looked at my watch."

"We want to show you something," Liam said. "Austin found it. We didn't want to tramp through Nenna's bedroom." The only ways to get in and out of Liam and Austin's room were by walking through Nenna and Granda's, and by taking the outdoor stairs from the porch. Liam and Austin probably snuck in and out of the house that way all the time.

"Can't you show it to us tomorrow?" Jocelyn asked.

"Nope. Surfing competition tomorrow," Austin said. "We're getting up early." He took a step back, out of the shadows, and I saw his face and a slice of his T-shirt in the moonlight. I tried to imagine him babysitting for me, buckling me carefully into a stroller. "Are you ready?" he asked. "Move your big head out of the way."

I held the screen up and ducked. Something hit the clapboard.

"Where'd you learn to throw like that?" Liam asked. "Why don't you let an athlete try it?"

"Give me two out of three," Austin said.

A light went on in Celia's bedroom.

"Hurry up," I said.

A few seconds later, something about the size of a walnut sailed through the window and past my head. Liam and Austin, underneath us, seemed to disappear.

I latched the screen while Jocelyn crawled under her bed to retrieve what they'd thrown: a wad of paper with a stone inside it. She smoothed the paper with her hands.

"What is it?" I whispered. Celia was probably prowling through the hall downstairs; we had to read by the light of the moon.

It seemed to be an article from the daily paper: *Miss Port Harbor Princess Wins College Scholarship*.

"Turn it over," I said.

135

On the other side was an ad for Port Harbor Realty. Someone had written *available August 15* across the picture of a squat yellow building, then circled it in pen. *Tired of yard work?* the ad asked. *Home maintenance a problem? We've got a new home for you in Port Harbor. Convenient, cozy, and comfortable: 21 Bay.*

CHAPTER SIXTEEN

☆

I sat on the edge of my bed in the dark and tried to think. I felt like someone had lifted the top of my head off and inserted an ugly brand-new idea into my brain.

Were Celia and Ellen selling the house? Was that why they'd cleaned out the attic? They were always talking about Granda's doctor appointments, and about Nenna and Granda both getting old. *Convenient, cozy, and comfortable*, the clipping said. It was probably some kind of nursing home.

"This doesn't make sense," I said. "There's no 'for sale' sign on the house." I tried not to imagine my Nenna and Granda in a place full of old people in wheelchairs, a double line of them in a cafeteria, wearing matching hospital gowns and eating soup.

Jocelyn had folded the clipping and put it away, and now she was rearranging things on her dresser: the lamp, the purse, the clock, the brush and comb, the jewelry box.

Where had Liam and Austin found the clipping? Did they know what it meant? How were we supposed to visit Nenna and Granda when we came to Port Harbor if they didn't have a house? Where would we stay?

Jocelyn nudged the jewelry box toward the lamp and wiped the clock on her nightgown.

I told her to get back into bed, and she actually listened to me. I tucked in her covers. The wooden floor creaked beneath my feet.

"Is everything all right up there?" It was Celia's voice, coming from the landing.

I froze and waited.

A few minutes later the light went off downstairs. I lay down in bed and listened to the ocean and to the sound of my cousin scratching in her sleep.

☆

Liam and Austin were already gone when I got up the next morning. I checked their bedroom, which was empty, and remembered what Liam had told me about the approach of a tidal wave—the feeling of something steadily disappearing under your feet.

Truth #42: Water freezes at thirty-two degrees Fahrenheit.

Nenna was reading the paper at the kitchen counter, and Granda was watching TV. There was some kind of storm off the southern coast of Argentina. "Would you like some toast, Thea?" Nenna asked. "Or maybe some oatmeal?"

"Toast would be good." I took the butter and the jam out of the refrigerator and got a plate from the shelf.

"The time has certainly gone fast, hasn't it?" Nenna asked. "You two will both be leaving before I know it."

Jocelyn was eating her breakfast. I watched her place a dozen yellow raisins in a perfect circle in her bowl of oatmeal.

"But we'll be back," I said. "Because you know I come back every summer." I waited for Nenna's reaction. "Since this is a great place to visit."

"That's very sweet, and I'm glad to hear it." Nenna put down her paper. "I hope you'll come back every year."

"As long as you have room for me, I will." I put two slices of bread in the toaster.

Nenna laughed. "How would I not have room for my oldest granddaughter? Or my youngest granddaughter, for that matter?"

We both looked at Jocelyn. She was stirring her oatmeal; the yellow raisins had been sucked into the mixture and had disappeared.

"I have some money for the two of you," Nenna said, taking a twenty-dollar bill from her bathrobe pocket. "For a haircut, with something left over. You don't mind, Thea?"

"No, that's okay." I studied the greenish portrait on

the front of the bill; Andrew Jackson's hair, I thought, and even his eyebrows could use a trim. The toaster dinged. I stuffed the twenty into my pocket. "Are you going to drive us there?" I asked.

"I wasn't planning to." Nenna put my toast on a plate. "It's only five or six blocks. Do you think you can get there on your own?"

The trike was waiting in the garage. "Sure," I said. "I guess we can do that." I turned around and saw my Granda smile.

☆

"Are you mad at me or something?" I asked when Jocelyn and I were on our way to get her hair cut. "You've been kind of quiet."

We rode past the Breakers, where Liam and Austin spent most of their time, slapping sandwiches together behind the carryout window.

"I have a headache." Jocelyn adjusted her bungee.

"Maybe a haircut will make it feel better." I steered around a pothole and rode up onto the sidewalk. "This must be it," I said, slowing down. "The Cut and Curl."

The women who worked in the beauty shop swiveled toward us when the little bells on the door jingled. They were all wearing smocks printed with pink and yellow scissors.

"Well, take a look at our new customer," said a

woman at the desk. "That appears to me to be a home haircut." Her mouth was bright red with lipstick and she was overweight, with upper arms the size of hams. She came out from behind the cash register and lifted Jocelyn's chin with her fingers. "But I know she'll look sweet when we're finished with her, won't she? What's your name, honey?"

"Jocelyn."

Truth #43: Gwen's little sister's name was Marie.

I expected Jocelyn to charm the women with her perfect politeness and her queen-among-the-peasants smile. But she picked at her glove.

"And who is this?" the ham-armed woman asked.

"My cousin Thea. She's taking care of me right now."

"Well, isn't *that* nice!" I knew what she was thinking: what kind of job was *Cousin Thea* doing if poor little Jocelyn had rashy skin and a prisoner's haircut?

"Scoot back in that chair, sweet pea." The woman—her name tag said *Lou*—tied a plastic apron around Jocelyn's neck and spritzed her hair with water.

I sat in a chair in the waiting area. The smell of hair dye and strawberry shampoo drifted up my nose. The table in front of me held a dozen different copies of *Spaniel*. One of the beauticians must have owned a show dog.

"There now! Doesn't she look precious!" All the

women in the shop oohed and aahed when the haircut was done. I stood up to see how things had worked out. Jocelyn's hair *was* kind of cute. She had a fuzzy blond inch-long bubble around her head. It looked like a dandelion puff.

Lou refused to charge us. "Not a single red cent," she said when I asked what we owed her. "You just take care of your little cousin. And I mean *good* care of her," she added.

"Okay, thanks," I mumbled. "I will."

☆

Truth #44: At Three Mile Creek there's a bend in the stream near a willow tree, and past the bend there's a sort of drainpipe that funnels the rain and snowmelt from a nearby suburb. Everyone knows about the pipe.

"Where are we going?" In the basket in front of me, Jocelyn opened her purse and put on a pair of pink sunglasses. She looked like a bug, I thought. Like a pink mosquito.

Truth #45: When my mother asked me where I'd been that afternoon back in February, I told her I'd been working on a research paper. "I was at the library," I said. Then I cupped my hands over my mouth because I thought I was going to be sick.

"Thea?" Jocelyn asked.

"Oh," I said. "We're going to the boardwalk."

We cruised past the post office and past DiCamillo's Deep-Fried Donuts and the big old rooming houses (ROOMS TO LET) with the old women rocking in the shade of their second-floor porches.

"I thought we weren't supposed to be riding around town," Jocelyn said.

I looked at her back while I pedaled, at the bony vertebrae like a row of marbles at the top of her spine. "Nenna basically told us to," I said. "She gave us money. We could get some pizza. And I thought we could stop by that realty office and ask for a map. Maybe we can find out where twenty-one Bay is."

Jocelyn didn't answer. We had reached the ramp. I could tell that my legs had gotten stronger; instead of getting off the trike to push, I kept pedaling. Two women stepped out of the way when I rang the bell.

It was a perfect beach day for midsummer: the sky was wide and flat and blue, dotted with parasailors who lifted off awkwardly from the water like enormous birds. Jocelyn and I rode past the house of mirrors, where a line of people clutching yellow tickets waited their turns to stumble toward each other's reflections. We rode past a caricature artist—a man who turned ordinary-looking people into strange-looking creatures with eyebrows like forests and teeth the size of playing cards. We rode past the taffy-pulling machine, the thick loops of candy like smooth sweet yarn, and into the revolving shadow of the Ferris wheel.

"There it is," I said. I stopped and tied up the trike. "Port Harbor Realty." I helped Jocelyn climb out of the basket (she was moving almost as slowly as Granda), then steered her through the human traffic on the boardwalk. The office was closed. A paper clock hanging in the window said, WILL RETURN AFTER LUNCH AT 1 P.M.

"You've got to be kidding." I shaded my eyes and peered into the office through the glass. "What time is it now? I think it's just after eleven-thirty. How long can it take them to eat lunch?"

Jocelyn ran a gloved finger along the window.

"I guess we'll have to come back later," I said. "Do you want something to eat?"

"No."

"Should we play Skee-Ball?"

Jocelyn turned toward the booth where the turbaned man was painting rice. What was the point of having a grain of white rice with your name written on it? "I want to ask for something," she said.

I noticed the wrinkle on her smooth pale forehead and realized that she wasn't looking at the name-on-rice man but at Madam Carla, whose tiny booth was next to his. "Let's not waste Nenna's money," I said. "Wouldn't you rather get a piece of pizza? Or ride the bumper cars?"

"I'm not hungry." The silver coins on Madam Carla's sign were shivering their message: KNOW YOUR FUTURE. "I need to ask her something," Jocelyn said.

It was strange, I thought: from a distance, Madam Carla had seemed unusual and mysterious. But once we were seated at her table, she looked like an ordinary tired person, with a narrow face and plain dark hair in a ponytail. She wore a long-sleeved black T-shirt that was tattered at the wrists. Without the rings on her fingers and the heavy makeup around her eyes, she would have looked like my math teacher, Mrs. Sullivan. I almost expected her to ask me how to multiply fractions.

"Five dollars each," she said. "Ten for the two of you." She didn't talk like a fortune-teller. She talked like a person from New Jersey. My mother always said that almost everyone from the state of New Jersey had a personal hatred for the vowel.

Jocelyn used her own money—her allowance—and insisted on buying a fortune for each of us. She counted out six wrinkled bills and four dollars in change, carefully stacking the coins on the table. Madam Carla didn't count them; she swept the money into a metal coin box as if performing a magic trick. "You two are related." She was looking at me. "But you aren't sisters."

"We're cousins," I told her. My legs were sticking to the vinyl chair.

"And you're here on vacation."

Jocelyn gave a little jolt of surprise, but I wasn't impressed. Ninety-nine percent of Port Harbor was in town on vacation.

"I think there's something you'd like to know," Madam Carla said. "Who's first?"

145

Jocelyn kept her gloved hands in her lap. I nudged her, but she didn't move, so I said, "I am," and I put my hand palm up on the table, where it lay on the black wrinkled fabric like a fish on a plate.

I thought again about Liam's description of a tidal wave, all that water churning and dragging itself out to sea.

"What's your name?" Madam Carla flattened my fingers gently. She traced a circle near my thumb.

"Thea," I said.

"Theodora," she said, as if correcting me. "A long life." Her breath smelled like cinnamon. "Good health—that's very clear—and probably a number of children, eventually. Two or three boys, I would say, if I were guessing." Her fingers moved lightly across my palm. "I see a successful marriage, as far as those things go. And a career in—what?" She looked up. Her eyes were gray, the color of stones at the bottom of a stream. "It could be advertising or journalism. Something that requires originality and imagination." She was studying my hand, smoothing my fingers. "But over here, this is unusual."

A man with an obscene word on his T-shirt stopped beside the table.

"It looks almost like grief," Madam Carla said. "I'm seeing—"

"How long does this take?" the T-shirt man asked.

Madam Carla slowly lifted her head and glared at

him. "There's no rushing the future," she said when he stalked away.

I had already pulled my hand off the table. "Jocelyn can have her turn now," I said.

Madam Carla raised one eyebrow; she didn't look like Mrs. Sullivan anymore. Jocelyn took off her gloves.

It had been a while since I'd seen her hands. Her skin was thick and looked painful. Her right hand was worse; it was callused and stained, the rash like a rough pink continent. Jocelyn stared at her lap. She was so short that her feet didn't touch the ground.

"Here are difficulties," Madam Carla said. I wasn't sure whether she was talking about Jocelyn's future or about her rash. She touched Jocelyn's fingers. She told her something about traveling to foreign lands and falling in love during some kind of harvest. It sounded like a fortune that anybody might have found in a fortune cookie.

I was wondering if Jocelyn's hand might be too hard to read. "You wanted to ask her something," I said, nudging my cousin. "You should go ahead and ask."

Jocelyn mumbled.

"I don't think she can hear you," I said.

Jocelyn spoke up. "I said, I want you to wait for me over there." She pointed to the custard booth.

"Me? You don't want me to sit here?"

"I'll come and get you," Jocelyn said.

I opened my mouth to object. Then I unstuck my legs from the vinyl chair and walked into the shade near the custard booth, where the man in the obscene T-shirt was complaining about the size of his waffle cone.

Truth #46: If you're going to drive a car across it, ice should be at least eight inches thick. If you're going to walk on it, you need four inches.

Jocelyn took a long time. I strained my ears. She and Madam Carla were talking and talking.

Finally Jocelyn stood up and put on her gloves. Madam Carla seemed to close up shop. She picked up her coin box, tucked it into a backpack, and wandered off in the direction of the Ferris wheel.

"How did it go?" I asked Jocelyn. "I guess you got your money's worth."

She nodded.

"Did you ask her where twenty-one Bay is?" I asked. "Or how we can find it?"

"I didn't need to ask her that," Jocelyn said. "I already know where it is."

CHAPTER SEVENTEEN

☆

"What do you mean, you know where it is?" I asked. "How long have you known?"

Jocelyn walked away, in the direction of the realty office. The paper clock was still in the window.

I grabbed her arm. "You really know where it is? So we don't have to wait for this place to open?"

"They have a map anyway," she said.

And in fact, they did; a fairly large map was taped up in the window, only partly obscured by a layer of grime. I walked over and studied it. Across the top it said, PORT HARBOR: NEW JERSEY'S FAVORITE FAMILY PLAYGROUND! Scattered here and there across it were cartoonlike drawings of the town's main attractions: the fire station, the jetty, the lighthouse, the boardwalk. The street names were written in large block letters, and without even looking for it, I found Bay Street (remarkably, it seemed to be located near the bay), a road about fifteen blocks from where we were standing.

"You think that's it?" I asked. "Twenty-one Bay? I guess it would be."

Jocelyn was fiddling with the strap on her purse.

"We can ride there and find out," I said. Something didn't seem right.

Jocelyn kicked at a nugget of caramel corn that had tumbled out of somebody's bucket. "What if they see us?" she asked.

"Celia and Ellen? They're not going to see us. They were only going to see us if we went back to the hotel."

Truth #47: If it had been someone else at the creek with Gwen—someone who didn't count things or care that they came out even— nothing bad would have happened.

Jocelyn walked away from the realty office, past the bakery and the paperback bookstore.

I followed her through a stream of people. "We're both going home soon, anyway," I said. "Jocelyn, wait for me. Where are you going?" I lost sight of her for a minute and felt almost desperate. "Jocelyn?" Dodging a man on a pair of crutches, I caught up to her in the doorway of the 99 Cent Store. EVERYTHING INSIDE ONLY 99 CENTS! The store window was streaked with dirt and sunlight, and it was crowded with inflatable sea serpents, Styrofoam surf-boards, shovels and buckets, books of postcards, and food.

Truth #48: I used to wish that someone would ask me, *What really happened to your best friend, Gwen?*

"You're out of breath," Jocelyn said, looking surprised. She had turned around.

"I'm all right," I told her. "I'm probably just thirsty." I wiped the sweat from my forehead. "Maybe we can get something to drink in here."

We walked into the 99 Cent Store, where the cashier, a bored-looking woman clutching a pencil between her teeth, was watching a miniature TV by the register. Beyond her, on the ceiling, were rows of long fluorescent bulbs that sent out a shuddering artificial light; everything smelled of plastic. We walked past dozens of bins full of flip-flops and yo-yos, Super Balls and baby bottles and Krazy Straws and squirt guns and coffee mugs and shampoo. Some of the toys were already broken. Two giant fans sent clumps of dust across the floor.

"I think we should go home after this," Jocelyn said. "We should go back to Nenna's."

I spotted a row of coolers humming in the back. "The soda's only ninety-nine cents. Do you want one?"

"No. Soda's bad for your teeth."

Feeling calmer than I had outside, I plucked a root beer from the cooler. When I turned around, Jocelyn was poking through a bin full of bathing caps, some of them the old-fashioned ladies' kind with chin straps, and rubber flowers all over. She picked up a daisy-covered cap.

"What did Madam Carla say to you?" I asked. "Did you ever get a real fortune?"

At the end of the aisle we were standing in, two girls were bouncing Super Balls next to a sign that said NO BOUNCING BALLS.

Jocelyn put down the bathing cap and examined a pyramid of toilet paper.

"Listen, Jocelyn," I said. I opened my root beer and took a sip, even though I hadn't paid for it yet. "I know you want to go back to Nenna's, but I think we should finish what we started."

Jocelyn picked up a bundle of handkerchiefs (3 FOR NINETY-NINE!) and a pair of swim goggles.

"Celia and Ellen aren't going to bother us. If we get in trouble, you can just tell them it was all my fault."

Jocelyn stopped near a bin full of masks. Some were the Batman kind, just a plastic oval with two eyeholes cut in the center; others were stained or battered versions of Snow White or Tinker Bell or Sleeping Beauty. Jocelyn leaned over and picked up a gorilla mask, then handed me a mask that looked like the Tin Man from *The Wizard of Oz*.

"Does that make sense? We'll ride past twenty-one Bay and find out what it is." I looked down at the cheap mask in my hand. "It's kind of early for Halloween," I said.

Jocelyn held the gorilla mask up to her face and

blinked at me through the little round eyeholes. "They aren't for Halloween," she said.

She left me standing in the aisle with my mouth half open and headed for the register, where the cashier was still watching TV. Jocelyn paid for the root beer and the masks, and we walked back into the glare of the afternoon.

A couple of gears were shifting in the back of my mind. "Tell me you aren't thinking what I think you're thinking," I said.

Three girls in shorts and brightly colored tube tops staggered past us, laughing. Their bleached hair gleamed like copper.

Truth #49: I still remember exactly what Gwen was wearing that day: tan corduroy pants and her favorite red sweater. I can still see her looking over her shoulder and laughing, dragging her backpack behind her along the ice.

We were heading for the trike. "You're the one who said you didn't want anyone to recognize us," Jocelyn said.

I paused, then nearly tripped over a knothole. "You might not appreciate this, Jocelyn," I said, "but it's already fairly unusual for me to be pedaling an old man's tricycle all over Port Harbor with a seven-year-old in the front basket. So I'm not going to wear a gorilla mask."

"You can be the Tin Man," Jocelyn said. "I don't mind being the gorilla."

Out on the beach, a lifeguard was standing at the edge of the water, pointing at someone on a raft and blowing her whistle.

"Are you coming or not?" Jocelyn asked.

Truth #50: That's what Gwen said to me at the creek: "Thea, are you coming or not?"

It appeared that I was. I was going to follow the path that lay in front of us, even though I felt nervous about where it led, and about the direction in which Jocelyn and I seemed to be going.

☆

Truth #51: The three worst mistakes I have made in my life so far all happened in the past five months:
- **going to Three Mile Creek with Gwen,**
- **making Gwen a promise I never should have made,**
- **agreeing to wear a gorilla mask (the Tin Man was too small) while pedaling a seven-year-old with a nearly shaved head on a giant tricycle through downtown Port Harbor, New Jersey.**

"Slow down," said the Tin Man.

The gorilla (me) was sweating like a pig. Do gorillas sweat? Pieces of fake gorilla fur were stuck to my forehead.

"This street is bumpy. You're going too fast." The Tin Man was a real complainer.

The gorilla slowed down and turned left at the corner. "I can barely see in this crazy thing. My entire face is falling off." In fact, my eyeholes seemed to be slipping.

I pulled over and we paused in the shade of a maple tree, two homely creatures under a leafy green umbrella. The Tin Man's head was an odd shape, I decided. It looked like a water tower with eyes.

I caught my breath and adjusted my mask. Bay Street was a narrow road with a column of houses on one side and a marsh on the other. Most of the yards were made of pebbles instead of grass. "It must be a couple of blocks ahead of us," I said.

Two boys on in-line skates rumbled by. One of them pointed at me. "Weird-looking monkey."

"I don't want anyone to see us," Jocelyn said. Her gloved hands gripped the sides of the basket.

I told her that no one was going to see us; she should just relax.

"We aren't supposed to be here," she said. "I want to go back to Nenna's."

"In a minute." I started to pedal.

Jocelyn grabbed the hand brake and squeezed it, and we jerked to a stop.

I pulled off my mask. I pulled hers off, too. "What is the matter with you?" I asked. The elastic had made a funny little line across the back of her haircut.

"You know what the secret is," Jocelyn said.

"What? I don't know what it is."

"You do," she insisted. Her voice was high and unsteady. "You talked to Liam. That's why he gave us that piece of paper."

"Jocelyn, I just asked him—you were sitting there next to me." I wasn't going to spend my time arguing with her. I started pedaling again, the gorilla mask dangling around my neck.

"You were supposed to tell me," Jocelyn said. She grabbed for the brake, but I swatted her hand away.

We rode past a man walking a dog on a leash; they had stopped to examine a cluster of cattails. They looked happy together, as if both of them thought strolling along a mosquito-infested marsh was a wonderful thing.

"I think you're a liar," Jocelyn said.

I told her to be quiet. We were almost there. "And stop squirming around," I said. "You're going to get hurt."

She unhooked her bungee cord while we coasted through an intersection. "I know where your notebook is," she said. "You keep it in the bathroom. In the back of the cabinet. I knew you weren't smoking cigarettes." She started to cry. "I know about your friend."

A ribbon of anger unrolled itself inside my chest.

Jocelyn was on one knee, almost standing up. "Everyone lies to me. You broke your promise." The trike was still moving.

All I could think was *You read my notebook*.

Jocelyn stepped on my wrist and tumbled against me, trying to get up.

I was about to warn her that she was going to fall when she caught the strap of her shoe in the basket. I lunged for her, managing to grab one of her ankles in its ruffled sock. But it was too late. The trike tipped. It seemed to turn on its side in slow motion, inch by inch, with Jocelyn trying to catch her balance but approaching the street. *How can a three-wheeler fall over?* I wondered. I reached for the brake but missed. Jocelyn's ruffled sock ended up, empty, in my hand. I wasn't sure how it happened or which came first: the trike hitting the pavement, the handlebars scraping against the street, the sudden pain shooting through my arm—or Jocelyn falling, headfirst, against the curb.

CHAPTER EIGHTEEN

☆

It didn't seem like a regular amount of blood—like the amount you usually see when someone gets injured. It seemed like a lot more than that. And it was sliding down Jocelyn's forehead and staining the cottony yellow of her hair.

"I hurt myself, Thea."

I dragged myself off the pavement, brushing some broken glass and gravel from my leg. Jocelyn was leaning against the curb. She touched her forehead and looked at her fingers, bright with blood.

She isn't dead, I told myself. *She can't be dead if she's talking.*

"I got something on my shirt." She rubbed at a patch of grease on her shoulder. A narrow ribbon of blood led from the cut on her forehead, down the side of her face, into her ear. She was so calm.

"Jocelyn, don't move," I said. "Can you stay right here? Right here in this spot?"

She looked at the blood on her fingers.

"I'll be right back," I said. "We need someone to help us. But you'll be okay. Everything's fine. You're going to be fine." I turned around, ready to run in any direction. The street was empty. The man and his dog had disappeared.

"I want to come with you," Jocelyn said.

"No, you need to stay here." I tried to wipe the blood from her face, but there was too much of it. How much blood did a person have? "I'm just going to knock on the door of that house over there. Do you see it? I'll be right back. You can sit here and watch me."

"I think I cut myself," she said. "Will you really come back?"

I wiped her face with my T-shirt and remembered how fast the temperature dropped at Three Mile Creek. "I'm sorry, Jocelyn." I stood up as if in a daze. *It can't be happening again*, I thought.

"Thea, wait," Jocelyn said.

But I turned around and started running. I felt the frozen creek closing in on me, and the weight of a thousand lies above my head.

Up the street, a car turned the corner. I sprinted toward it, waving my arms; I was screaming and shouting. The car pulled over. Celia was driving, and Ellen was beside her in the passenger seat. A few seconds later, they were running toward us as fast as they could.

☆

At the tiny Port Harbor Clinic, they put Jocelyn in one room and me in another. Nenna and Phoebe (carrying Ralph) had somehow appeared and were both with Jocelyn; Celia and Ellen were filling out medical forms in the hall. ("You're using a pencil for that?" Celia asked. "Do you think this is elementary school?")

For a while I sat in the examining room by myself and counted stripes in the carpet; then a nurse came in and took my blood pressure and my temperature ("Normal," she said) and cleaned Jocelyn's blood off my arm. She also gave me a blanket because I was shivering. I didn't feel cold, but my entire body was shaking; there were little earthquakes happening up and down my spine.

Jocelyn had seemed okay during the trip to the clinic: Celia and Ellen had been talking to her. But what if she *seemed* fine, and then later she went into a coma?

If anything happened to her, it would be my fault: instead of babysitting the way a normal person would, I had perched a seven-year-old on the front of a giant tricycle, without a helmet, and strapped her in place with a bungee cord. And even though Celia and Ellen had warned me not to take her past the nursing home, the place where my Nenna and Granda were probably going to be shipped off to die, I'd done it anyway, and of course Jocelyn had gotten upset and tried to leap off the trike. And now my Grumman relatives would all hate me, and the house would be sold, and I would never be able to set foot in Port Harbor again.

I sat on the paper-covered table and shook.

"So. Let's see here. You're Theodore. Or Theodora." A white-jacketed doctor had breezed into the room, followed by the nurse, who was holding a tray. "Can I see that arm?"

"What arm?" I asked.

He smiled, took hold of my wrist, and turned it over. There was a jagged cut below my elbow. I hadn't known it was there, but now that I saw it, it hurt. I made the mistake of looking at it when he bent my elbow; the skin on my arm opened like an ugly mouth.

"Do you know how Jocelyn is?" I asked. "Have you seen her?"

"Hold still. This might sting for a minute." The doctor unwrapped a needle that looked like it was long enough to go through my entire body twice.

"I don't need any shots," I said, pulling away. "I just want to see Jocelyn."

"You don't want stitches without anesthetic." The doctor seemed to be debating with himself: *Should I give her stitches without anesthetic?*

"I don't want stitches at all." The world as I knew it was falling apart, and now this perfect stranger was determined to stab me with a needle.

I didn't like needles. I didn't like the needly way they looked—their terrible, pointed, glinting shape.

"Just try to relax," the doctor said. He made some sort

of gesture to the nurse, something that probably meant *You strap her down and I'll stick this thing through her.* Maybe it was a truth serum, I thought. It would serve me right. I wouldn't be able to lie anymore.

The nurse stood beside me and blocked my view as something horrible and sharp pierced the cut on my arm. "Is your whole family here?" the doctor asked. "Don't make a fist."

I could hear someone arguing in the hall. Was it Austin? Or Liam? Whose family was the doctor talking about?

A few minutes later I felt a tugging near my elbow, as if someone was sewing me, actually stitching through my skin with a needle and thread. I saw puckers of light around the edges of the room.

Someone knocked on the door, and the nurse answered. "I don't think we're ready for visitors yet," she said, but Nenna probably didn't hear her.

She was pushing Jocelyn toward us in a wheelchair. Phoebe and Liam were behind them. Jocelyn had a circle of gauze around her forehead. She almost looked like the man who painted names on rice.

I stared at the wheelchair. This was what I had done to her. "Jocelyn, are you paralyzed?" I asked.

"No." She moved her legs. "They just want me to sit here."

Celia and Ellen crowded into the doorway. I thought I saw Austin somewhere behind them.

Jocelyn wheeled herself toward me. "I'm sorry about your notebook," she said. "I only meant to read a page."

"We still need a few stitches here," the doctor said.

"But then I wanted to find out what happened." Everyone was quiet for at least fifteen seconds. It was probably a Grumman world record.

"Tell me the truth," Jocelyn said. "What happened to your friend? How did she die?"

CHAPTER NINETEEN

☆

Truth #52: Three Mile Creek is fifteen feet wide, and it cuts through a tangle of poplar trees.

Truth #53: The water in the creek isn't very deep. When the weather was hot, in the summer, I used to sit on a wide, flat rock and let my legs dangle in the current.

Truth #54: I used to love the way the water curled along the bank like liquid silver. On the bottom of the creek there are strange green plants like boneless fingers, and the underwater stones are round and slippery with moss.

Truth #55: This is a story I don't want to tell. I promised Gwen that I would never tell it.

Truth #56: Some days in the winter, after school, the ice was full of little kids playing hockey. The creek was wide enough to play three kids on a side. But when Gwen and I climbed down the bank that day, the ice was empty, a fat white snake.

Truth #57: Of course I was the one who invented the game.

Truth #58: The game went like this: I took the bag of Monopoly markers from my jacket pocket, where I always kept them, and Gwen and I lined ourselves up beside the big gray rock.

Truth #59: My favorite marker was the shoe. Gwen's was the race car. The idea was to lose something you loved and then find it again.

Truth #60: The sun had been out all day. Gwen wasn't wearing a scarf or a hat.

Truth #61: I reached into the bag and counted the pieces: the shoe, the race car, the hat, the dog, the iron, the ship, the thimble, the cannon, the soldier, and the wheelbarrow. Ten. It had to be ten. I closed my eyes and threw them. They made a quiet clattering sound when they hit the ice.

Truth #62: Ice always has cracks in it. Even ice in the ice cube tray, if you look at it closely, is full of cracks.

Truth #63: "Come on, let's start," Gwen said. The object was to be the first person to find five of the markers and make it back to the big gray rock. And we had to touch the rock every time we found a marker.

165

Truth #64: I stole the markers from Nenna's Monopoly game after losing to Liam about two years before. I never told her. (I'm sorry, Nenna.)

Truth #65: Sliding on outdoor ice isn't easy. The ice on Three Mile Creek is bumpy and uneven, full of frozen snow. Sometimes you'll find pennies that Richard Lemon and his younger brothers have dropped and spat on, creating copper constellations under their feet.

Truth #66: Gwen said, "Go!" and we started running. It wasn't getting dark yet, but the color in the day had faded. The sky was gray and looked as if someone had draped it over the trees like a giant tarp.

Truth #67: Even before we reached the first markers, I could feel someone watching us.

Truth #68: Gwen had been my friend since kindergarten. Her parents liked me. Her mother used to say I was "full of beans."

Truth #69: I found the hat, and Gwen found the race car. We both turned around and ran back to the rock, dodging tree roots and low-hanging branches. I skidded toward the opposite bank and grabbed the iron (where was the shoe?) while Gwen found the soldier. Laughing and slamming into each other, we both touched the rock. I found the thimble and Gwen found the ship. We still had to look for the wheelbarrow and the cannon, the dog and the shoe.

Truth #70: That's the last good memory I have of Gwen.

Truth #71: Gwen's sister, Marie, was supposed to be sick that day; she had stayed home from school. But there she was on the ice behind us.

Truth #72: I used to wish I had a sister. But Gwen always said I shouldn't wish for a younger one.

Truth #73: Marie was nine.

Truth #74: We should have just finished our game and gone home.

Truth #75: "You're not supposed to be here, Marie," Gwen said.

Truth #76: A drowning person, because she is desperate, can easily drown somebody else.

Truth #77: Marie stuck out her tongue and picked up a pine branch and started using it like a broom. She was sweeping the ice, scattering twigs and stones and dirt and the four metal markers we still needed to find. I saw one of the markers zip past and tried to grab it but missed.

Truth #78: "You have to pick those up," Gwen said. She grabbed Marie by the collar of her jacket.

Truth #79: I found the wheelbarrow right away. Then in a clump of leaves downstream, I found the cannon and the dog. The shoe—it was really a tiny silver boot, with a wrinkle just above the heel—was about three feet from the drainage pipe. "Marie has to go get it," Gwen said. "Tell her, Thea." I looked at the pipe.

Truth #80: I could have bought a new Monopoly game. I could have borrowed someone else's pieces.

Truth #81: But I wanted that shoe. Marie looked at me. "You'd better go get it," I said. Somehow I knew she would do what I asked her. Marie probably weighed about seventy pounds.

Truth #82: Like a crack of thunder but sharper and quicker. Like a giant pop-top opening.

Truth #83: Even though I had never heard that sound before, I knew what it was.

Truth #84: Marie disappeared into the ice, the gray water surging up around her. One minute she was standing on the creek in front of us; the next she was a blur of freezing water, ice, and mud. I knew that her shoes and her heavy jacket would weigh her down.

Truth #85: My mother had signed me up several months earlier for the Red Cross first aid and emergency class. That was the first thought that came to me: *I have taken the Red Cross emergency class.*

Truth #86: I knew how to stop, drop, and roll. I knew how to perform the Heimlich maneuver. Gwen was screaming. I knew that ABC stood for *airway, breathing, and circulation.*

Truth #87: Marie came up through the ice several times, flailing her arms, but she couldn't find anything to hold on to. Her hands clawed the surface. I couldn't move.

Truth #88: What is the myth about the Greek or Roman girl who gets stolen into the underworld, and because she is missing, spring will never come?

Truth #89: *She just needs to put her feet on the bottom,* I thought. *The water is shallow.*

Truth #90: I still wasn't moving. *Persephone,* I thought. That was the Greek girl's name. We had read about her in Mr. Hermes' class the year before.

Truth #91: We needed a rope. Gwen was shouting that it was all my fault. "It was your idea to go to the creek," she screamed. "It was your stupid game."

Truth #92: I should have been looking for tree limbs or boards—something we could use as a life preserver. *I have just killed a person,* I thought.

Truth #93: In my nightmares Marie is still flailing underneath us, her dark hair tangling like a mermaid's. Her eyes are searching for the surface. The world is a silver smear above her head.

Truth #94: "You can never tell anyone what happened," Gwen sobbed. Her face was white. "This was your fault, Thea. You have to promise." We were splattered with mud and freezing water.

"But it was an accident," Jocelyn said. "You couldn't save her."

Truth #95: I promised.

"Did you go to her funeral?" The room was crowded but quiet. Even the doctor and the nurse were listening.
"No," I said.
"Why not?"

Truth #96: Marie is alive.

CHAPTER TWENTY

☆

When we got back to the house, I didn't want anyone to talk to me. I would have gone to the beach to be alone, but it started to rain. I ended up in Nenna and Granda's garage.

About an hour went by. Maybe it was two hours. I was sitting on a giant coil of hose between the lawn mower and the volleyball net. I was thinking about how I had almost killed two people—and now everyone knew it. Spiders were getting ready to use me as an anchor in their webs.

Celia opened the door. "I thought I might find you here," she said. "I suppose you knew we were looking for you."

I nodded. Maybe they were getting ready to vote me out of the family.

"Jocelyn's fine, you know." Celia pushed a bag of

weed killer against the wall with her foot. "No concussion. No bleeding from the ears or mismatched pupils. Head wounds tend to bleed a lot. How's your arm?"

"It's okay." Actually, it hurt, but I didn't feel like I deserved to say so.

"Can we get you anything?" Celia opened the door a little wider and I saw Ellen standing next to her. She had her hands on her hips, but she waved a few fingers.

I waved back.

"I think we'll sit down for a while," Celia said. "We'll take a load off. Do you mind?" She didn't wait for an answer but pulled two folding chairs off a hook on the wall and set them up on the cement in the doorway. It was starting to get dark. Celia pulled the string that turned on the lightbulb over our heads, and then she and Ellen sat down, facing me.

"That hose doesn't look very comfortable," Ellen said.

I told her it was fine.

"We spoke to your parents." She started arranging the croquet balls on their metal stand. "It seemed like a good idea to call them, since you ended up in the hospital."

"What did they say?"

"Oh, they had a few questions. How did it happen and so on, and why were you riding an ancient tricycle on the other side of town, and why were you so badly supervised. That sort of thing. We told them you would fill them in on the details later."

"Oh. Okay." There was a click from the croquet balls.

"Here's what I don't understand," Celia said. "How did you figure it out?"

I shifted around on the garden hose. "You mean twenty-one Bay?"

I had planned to argue with them when we had this discussion. I had planned to accuse them of treating Nenna and Granda badly. But who was I to accuse them of anything when I had nearly killed Jocelyn? "We saw you at the realtor's," I said. "And then we saw the key with the address on it. We overheard you talking and pretty soon one thing led to another."

"So Jocelyn knew," Celia said. She leaned back in her chair. "I wondered."

"I'm so angry at Trisha I could spit," said Ellen. She set the final croquet ball in place. "I told her it was ridiculous not to tell them."

"She wanted to wait." Celia sighed. " 'Irreconcilable differences.' I could have told them that when they got engaged."

"When who got engaged?" I asked. "What are you talking about? I thought we were talking about the nursing home."

Above our heads, the lightbulb flickered.

"What nursing home?" Celia blinked.

"The one you're sending Nenna and Granda to. At twenty-one Bay."

My aunts looked at me oddly.

"Twenty-one Bay isn't a nursing home," Ellen said. "It's an apartment building." She picked up a croquet ball, weighed it in her hand, and put it back down. She glanced at Celia. "And it isn't for your Nenna and Granda. The apartment's for Trisha."

"Trisha?" The coils of the hose pinched my leg. "You mean *Jocelyn's* mom, Trisha? Why would Aunt Trisha need an apartment?" The lightbulb sputtered once more, and suddenly we were sitting in the dark. "Is she moving out?"

The light came on again, just long enough for me to see Celia and Ellen turn toward each other. Then we were plunged back into darkness.

"Are Trisha and Gray—" I said. "Do you mean—Are they getting divorced?"

"I thought that was what we were talking about," Celia said.

A door seemed to open inside my brain. "But they're on vacation," I said. "Who gets divorced when they're on vacation?"

"Trisha's leading a tour." Ellen's voice came from the doorway. "And Gray had a conference. Each of them wanted some time on their own before—"

"They wanted to explain it to Edmund and Jocelyn together," Celia said, "when Trisha gets back. Ellen and

I told them it didn't make sense. And we'll remind them of that when we call them later. People always think kids won't pick up on this kind of thing."

"So Jocelyn knows." I shook my head. "She figured it out. She didn't think it was a nursing home."

"She must have suspected something," Celia said. "And then when the two of you started following us—"

"We've been trying to get the apartment ready for them," Ellen said. "We were driving over there when we saw you. There are three small bedrooms—"

"That's why she didn't want to see the building," I said. "She must have recognized the address. She knew."

Ellen was grappling with something on a shelf in the corner: a flashlight. She pushed a button and lit up a circle of cement at our feet. "By the way," she said. "Jocelyn told us what happened. It wasn't only your fault. She shouldn't have tried to stand up when the trike was moving."

"If it makes you feel any better," Celia said, "Ellen dropped your father down a flight of stairs when he was a baby."

"And I seem to remember," Ellen added, "that you nearly killed Phoebe several times. You convinced her to hide in the neighbors' trash can."

"That's right, I'd forgotten about that," Celia said.

I stared at the circle of light between us and remembered the hole in the ice, Marie plunging through it. When we'd finally pulled her onto the bank, she had gasped for air like a fish on a hook. We took off our jackets and wrapped her up; her hair was dripping with mud and leaves. She probably hadn't been underwater as long as it had seemed.

"I should have made Jocelyn wear a helmet," I said.

Celia agreed that wearing a helmet was important.

"And I should have told my parents what happened to Marie." I had never wanted anyone to find out what had happened at the creek, but now that they knew, I felt lighter, easier. I felt as if my body had more room inside my skin.

There was a thump from above. "What's everyone doing upstairs?" I asked.

Ellen stood up and brushed herself off. "More of the usual. When we left, there were a couple of card games going on, and the TV and the radio were both playing full blast, and it was impossible to hear yourself think."

"It's what you'd expect," Celia said. "Havoc and chaos with a little mayhem. Your Nenna's making a big pot of soup, and we're going to eat a late dinner."

I stood up and took a deep breath. The air in the garage was damp and soft. "So Nenna and Granda aren't moving," I said. "They're staying here. And Granda's okay?"

Ellen turned off her flashlight. "People don't get better when they have Parkinson's," she said.

Celia folded the chairs. "He's going to keep slowing down."

It was hard to imagine my Granda getting any slower, but I knew they were telling me the truth. The truth has a weight, a certain shape you can recognize. And it comes in only one color.

"Do you think he'd mind that we borrowed his trike?" I asked.

"I think he'd be very happy to hear it," Ellen said. She closed the garage door behind us, and we went upstairs.

CHAPTER TWENTY-ONE

☆

The conversation I had with my parents was fairly awkward. I told them that my elbow was okay (six stitches), and that Jocelyn's head seemed to be all right also (eleven stitches). Then I apologized for being a liar and a terrible disappointment to them, and I said I was sorry that I had almost murdered someone—twice.

"You aren't a disappointment," my father said. "Besides, I think Ellen almost killed me once. She dropped me down a flight of stairs when I was a kid."

They asked me to tell them exactly what had happened at Three Mile Creek, and I found that it wasn't as hard to tell the story the second time.

My parents didn't say anything for a moment. I wondered whether they wanted to disown me. Then I heard my father say, "It's all right, honey. Thea's fine," and I realized that my mother was crying.

"I'm so sorry we didn't know," she finally said. "This happened to you months ago—*months*—and you didn't tell anyone. You could have told me." She said that being alone with the truth for so long must have been very hard.

"It *was* hard," I said. The lies I had told weren't very good company.

My father asked whether I wanted to come home early. "We can change your plane ticket," he said. "You can come home tomorrow."

I'd been facing the wall, for privacy (everyone in the kitchen was pretending not to listen in), but now I turned around. Celia and Ellen and Phoebe and Nenna were all getting in each other's way in the kitchen, Austin and Liam were playing cards with Edmund, and Granda was watching the Weather Channel. Jocelyn, a bandage wrapped around her head, was sitting by herself in a rocking chair on the porch. I told my parents not to change the ticket. I needed a few more days in Port Harbor before I went home.

☆

"Hey there," I said, opening the sliding door to the porch.

Jocelyn didn't turn around. "Look: I used that new cream. It made my skin better." She held up her hands. I thought they still looked awfully scaly, but at least she wasn't wearing gloves.

I wasn't sure what to say. *I'm sorry your parents are getting divorced. I'm sorry they lied to you. I'm sorry I lied to you. But you really shouldn't have read my notebook.*

Truth #97: I'll have to tell Gwen that I broke my promise.

"I never told you what the fortune-teller said to me." Jocelyn rocked back and forth.

"I guess you didn't." I was watching the stars begin to display themselves over the ocean.

"I asked her if you would invite me to Minnesota," Jocelyn said. "And she told me you would."

"That was your fortune? You could have just asked *me* that," I said.

Jocelyn tucked her hands into her armpits. "Also, she said if you don't invite me, I should ask your mother, and she'll make you invite me, because I'm your cousin."

"You don't have to force me," I said. "I'll invite you. I'm inviting you now."

Truth #98: I don't mind that Jocelyn's going to visit. If I don't see her for a while, I'll probably forget how annoying she is and even want her to come.

"Thea?"

"What?"

"Do you think you'll ever be friends again? You and that girl? The one who had the sister who almost died?"

"Probably not," I said.

We had tried at first. I had called Gwen a couple of times, and then she had called me, but the afternoon at the creek seemed like a line that had been drawn between us. About two weeks later the ice was gone, and Gwen started walking home from school with Kara Rockcastle, whose family had a trampoline in their yard and a nanny who let the kids do whatever they wanted. She almost seemed like a different person. And so did I.

Austin poked his head through the sliding door and said Nenna wanted someone to set the table. "And I'm going to take a shower," he said. "So it needs to be you."

Jocelyn followed me indoors. "Have you finished your notebook?"

"No." I got the dishes out of the cabinet. Counting Ralph, there would be twelve of us for dinner.

"I think you should finish it." Jocelyn counted out the napkins. "You said you were going to discover something."

I found a sheet of paper on the counter. It was an ordinary piece of loose-leaf. I picked it up.

"I wonder what it will be?" Jocelyn asked. "Maybe you'll discover something secret that no one ever knew before."

I started tearing the sheet of paper into twelve small pieces.

Truth #99: I have always wanted to set up a round of the dinner game.

"Or maybe you'll discover another planet."

I was scribbling names. There were so many different combinations, so many interesting possibilities. I remembered what my mother had told me in the airport: *You might find out something new about who you are.*

"Maybe you'll discover a cure for a disease so that you can help Granda," Jocelyn said.

I glanced around at the circle of plates. Soon the table would be full of Grummans, arguing and shouting and eating and guessing.

"Where do you want to sit, Jocelyn?" I asked.

Truth #100: I already know who we are.

ABOUT THE AUTHOR

Julie Schumacher is the author of *Grass Angel*, a PEN Center USA Literary Award Finalist for Children's Literature, and *The Chain Letter*, both published for young readers by Delacorte Press. She is also the author of numerous short stories and two books for adults, including *The Body Is Water*, an Ernest Hemingway Foundation/PEN Award Finalist for First Fiction and an ALA Notable Book of the Year.

An associate professor of English at the University of Minnesota, Julie Schumacher lives with her husband and their two daughters in St. Paul.